By Cynthia Keller

AN AMISH GIFT

A PLAIN & FANCY CHRISTMAS

AN AMISH CHRISTMAS

An Amish Gift

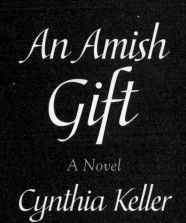

An Amish
Gift

A Novel

Cynthia Keller

BALLANTINE BOOKS · NEW YORK

Copyright © 2012 by Cynthia Steckel

Published in the United States by Ballantine Books, an imprint of The Random House Publishing Group, a division of Random House, Inc., New York.

Ballantine and colophon are registered trademarks of Random House, Inc.

Library of Congress Cataloging-in-Publication Data
Keller, Cynthia.
An Amish gift : a novel / Cynthia Keller.
p.   cm.
ISBN 978-0-345-53813-0 (hardcover : acid-free paper)—
ISBN 978-0-345-53814-7 (ebook)
1. Amish—Pennsylvania—Fiction.   2. Christmas stories.   I. Title.
PS3572.I263A85 2012
813'.54—dc23   2012028726

Printed in the United States of America on acid-free paper

www.ballantinebooks.com

2 4 6 8 9 7 5 3 1

First Edition

Book design by Liz Cosgrove

For Jenna and Carly,
wherever you may go in life,
my love goes with you

Acknowledgments

Thank you to my wonderful editor, Linda Marrow, and the other people on her staff who have provided me with so much support, including Junessa Viloria and Penelope Haynes.

A big hug to my supremely talented agent and cherished friend, Victoria Skurnick.

As always, I am grateful to my husband, Mark, with whom I have traveled so many roads in life. I love you.

An Amish Gift

Chapter 1

"What do you say, Scout? You want to stop for something to eat?"

Jennie Davis swiveled around as far as she could manage in the front passenger seat to direct her question to the black mutt with white paws and intelligent-looking black eyes, wedged in between the two teenagers in the back of the Honda.

Thirteen-year-old Willa rolled her eyes. "Mom, why do you always do that? Do you actually expect Scout to answer you?"

Jennie smiled at her daughter. "What makes you think he doesn't?"

Tim, her fifteen-year-old son, spoke with exaggerated bewilderment. "Now, why would we think that? Maybe because that would make you the first person in history to have a conversation with a dog?"

Shep Davis glanced over at his wife. "After Scout has expressed his preference, could I get a vote? I'd like to stop for some coffee."

Jennie rested her hand on her husband's arm. "You know what? Even if Scout says no, we're stopping for your coffee."

He smiled. "Wow. I'm honored."

Jennie smiled back. "On the day Scout drives for seven hours, he can decide when to stop, too."

"She actually is insane." Tim looked down at the dog by his side. "Don't you think so?"

Scout only crossed his two front paws on the seat and rested his head on them.

Jennie nodded, satisfied. "You didn't think he would talk against me, did you?"

Willa smacked her hand to her forehead in a theatrical show of exasperation.

"Hey, more cows." Shep gestured in the direction of a small herd, tails swishing as they stood patiently in the hot August sun.

"It'd be nice to have our own cows," Willa said.

Jennie swung around in her seat again. "Honey, we're not going to have room for that. Not that we'd know how to take care of a cow, anyway. But remember, this isn't a farm—it's a regular house. With a lot of farms around the area."

Jennie figured she was safe in making this limited assertion, though she hesitated to say anything more. They had seen only an old photograph of the house, taken from across the road. Online maps revealed that it wasn't large, but they knew it contained at least three bedrooms, which was one more bed-room than they'd ever had.

"Even with just one cow, we could have our own milk." Willa was getting excited by the idea. "It'd be all natural and stuff."

Tim groaned. "Listen to this. Wilma, do you know how hard it is to take care of a cow? You getting up in the middle of the night to milk it?"

"Don't call me Wilma!" She had always hated her brother's nickname for her. "And don't worry, nobody expects you to get up to milk it. Hard work is definitely not for you."

"No, you're going to do it, right? The person who's afraid of her own shadow, just going to take charge of that two-million-pound animal."

"Will you two stop?" Shep asked in annoyance.

Jennie was pleased to see an opportunity for distraction. "Look, there's a place for coffee."

"Can I get some?" Willa asked.

"We've gone over this," Shep said to her. "No coffee at your age. The end."

"You can get something else, though," Jennie threw in. As long as it's not too expensive, she silently added. It was hard to know how long they would have to make their money last, and it was little enough to begin with.

After arming themselves with coffee and soda, they contin-ued on the last leg of the trip, another forty-five minutes to the heart of Lancaster County. Jennie and Shep commented on the beauty of the countryside, admiring the wide-open fields dotted by clapboard houses and storybook-perfect farms. The children were far more intrigued by the occasional horses and buggies they passed, staring at the Amish men and women sitting in the open wagons. Willa waved at them and was sometimes rewarded with a return wave from a woman or a man in a straw hat.

"That is beyond . . ." Tim's words were lost as he rolled down the window to stick his head out and get a better view of a man and a boy in a closed buggy.

"Stop gawking," Shep said. "They're people, not exhibits for your amusement."

Tim settled back in his seat. "If they didn't expect people to gawk, they wouldn't go out like that."

Shep glanced at his wife, who was consulting a map. "I can't believe what I'm hearing." He looked in the rearview mirror at his son. "I'm ashamed that you would say such a thing."

"Naturally," Tim snapped back. "When are you not ashamed of me?"

Jennie interrupted. "According to this, we should be coming up to our street soon. But I don't know whether we go right or left."

No one said anything in the few minutes it took to get to the next intersection.

"This is it," Jennie said. "There's the street sign, that little one."

"Okay, we'll try this way first." Shep made a wide turn to minimize any disturbance to the contents of the U-Haul trailer attached to their car. He drove slowly down the narrow road so they could check the mailboxes.

Willa spotted it first. "I think that says 225. See?" She pointed, keeping her other arm securely wrapped around Scout.

The numbers were partially worn away from the old mailbox attached to a tilting wooden post. Shep pulled into the driveway, drove a few yards, then stopped so they could get a broad view of the house. He turned off the ignition. The four of them stared at the sight before them in dismayed silence. It was a small saltbox half hidden behind long-untended bushes.

A fresh beginning, Jennie reminded herself. This will be a fresh beginning. Inwardly, she groaned. They could deal with the overgrown front yard, but the driveway desperately needed repaving, and the house's paint was visibly peeling. She spotted a number of broken shutters at several windows; some were missing altogether. The whole thing was just sad-looking, she couldn't help thinking. Nor did it bode well for what they might find inside.

Her son was first to break the silence, his tone threatening. "This better not be the place."

Jennie tried to keep her voice cheerful. "It's the place, all right."

Her husband glanced over at her. "We passed all those big, open fields. I kind of hoped . . ."

She put a hand on his. "I know."

Tim interrupted. "We left Lawrence for this?"

"Mom?" Willa's voice was tremulous. "Mom, is this for real?"

"Come on, kids." Jennie turned to them a final time. "It's

not so bad. I know it's not what you probably dreamed of, but we'll fix it up."

"What we 'dreamed of'?" Tim snorted. "This place is a dump."

"But it's our dump. All ours, free and clear."

"Not sure what kind of person would pay for this," her husband muttered under his breath.

"Shep, that's not really helpful." Jennie spoke softly but forcefully. "We need to have a good attitude."

"In front of the children, you mean?" Tim turned to his sister. "Yes, by all means, let's delude the children. It's not as if they're smart enough to see for themselves that this is even worse than Lawrence."

"That's enough out of you," Shep snapped at him.

Jennie watched her husband get out of the car and slam the door. He was shaking his head, whether about the house or his son, she wasn't sure.

"Mom, Tim is right. This is way worse than our house," Willa pointed out in alarm.

True, Jennie thought, but she only smiled. "Nonsense. This place is ours, and our old place wasn't. We can make it into anything we want." She opened her car door. "And we'll make it wonderful."

Getting out to stand where the children couldn't see her, she let her smile fall away. Finding out four months ago that Shep was inheriting a house had felt like winning the lottery. It meant they could leave their half of the cramped two-family house they had been renting for nearly ten years and move into a place that was theirs alone. Even more incredible, it was completely paid off. It came to them courtesy of a cousin of Shep's mother whom no one had even known about. His mother had been dead for some twenty-five years, but apparently, this cousin, Bert Howland, had been a close playmate of hers when they were children. His wife had died long ago, and he had no other living heirs, so he'd named Shep the sole beneficiary of both his home and the bicycle shop he had operated for over thirty years.

They had been astounded by this act of generosity from someone who may have been a family member but was a total stranger to them. It had even come at the perfect moment, with Shep having lost his most recent job, and the two of them coming to the end of what little savings they had. Though it wasn't an easy move to make, there wasn't anything holding them in Lawrence, the small Massachusetts town where they had both grown up. There were few jobs to be had there, and it had gotten grimmer with every passing year. Yet they had never considered leaving, certainly not to go to a strange part of the country where they didn't know a soul. The children were in shock about being dragged off to Lancaster County, which might as well have been the moon as far as they were concerned; characteristically, Tim was furious, Willa quietly miserable. Still, that was all beside the point. By some miracle, they had been given a reprieve from financial calamity through a place to live and a business handed to them with no strings attached.

The heat of the afternoon was oppressive. Jennie gazed at

the large damaged patches on the roof of the house, wishing she could feel the same gratitude toward this mysterious relative that she had felt earlier. At the moment, what she felt was dread as she contemplated the work ahead of them. Thank goodness she and Shep could do most of the physical labor themselves; he was a magician at fixing things, and she would help. Still, they couldn't afford to buy the materials they would need. More important, he had a new business to run, and she had to presume that it would demand most of his time and energy.

Well, she thought, they would simply find a way through. Somehow it would work out.

Scout bounded out of the car, thrilled to be released from his confinement. He gave a few joyful barks, then raced over to follow Shep, tail wagging, as Willa came to join Jennie.

"Let's see what it's like inside," Jennie said. She bent over to peer at Tim, who was still in the backseat, his arms folded, his expression enraged. "You going to stay in there all day? I'd have thought you spent enough hours in the car."

"I'd rather live here than there."

She sighed. "Okay, you've made your point. Now come on out."

Making no effort to hide his annoyance, he threw open the door and emerged. Tall and broad-shouldered, he looked re-markably like his father, with the same sandy-colored hair and hazel eyes. The only thing missing was the dimple on Shep's left cheek, which, to Jennie, only made her husband more handsome when he smiled. Willa resembled Jennie, both of them with brown eyes and long brown hair usually tied back in a low ponytail.

Tim leaned back against the car, hands shoved in his jeans pockets, refusing to look anywhere but at the ground.

"Fine, be that way," Jennie said in resignation, turning away and gesturing to her daughter to follow.

Her husband was already at the side of the house, frowning as he knelt to inspect the foundation. Jennie reached for the screen door, pleasantly surprised to find that it appeared relatively new. That was one less thing they had to worry about, she thought. She would be grateful for small favors.

Inside the narrow front hall, she wasn't at all surprised to see a covering of dust practically everywhere. At best, no one would have been here to clean since Bert Howland had died, although, judging from the entryway's appearance, it had been a lot longer than six weeks. She took a quick tour of the cramped downstairs. Kitchen, half-bathroom, living room, dining room—all small, all apparently unchanged in decades. Dark, heavy wooden furniture did nothing to make the tiny rooms seem any larger. The living room had a rug with areas almost completely worn through in spots. She guessed that the old rocking chair next to a small table and black gooseneck lamp was where the house's inhabitant had spent much of his time; it held a flattened, faded seat cushion, and a thin pillow with a grimy gray pillowcase offered minimal back support. A coffee cup rested on the table. She leaned forward just far enough to look in, relieved to see it had a dried coffee stain on the bottom but was otherwise empty. In the kitchen, she found outdated appliances, rust on the stove and sink faucets, the refrigerator's door handle broken. Everything looked grimy.

Scout came bounding into the room, wagging his tail at the sight of her.

"So, what do you think?" she asked the dog, kneeling down to scratch behind his ears. "Could have been worse, you know. Way worse." Hearing Willa's footsteps coming down the narrow staircase, she called out, "In here, honey."

Her daughter appeared in the doorway, looking pale. "I checked out the bedrooms."

Jennie stood. "And?"

"They're, like, the size of shoe boxes. I mean, I'm not even kidding. There are two that are a joke, and I don't think anybody's been in them for about a hundred years. There's a third one, the big one, if you want to call it that, but don't bother. That's where he must have slept." She wrinkled her nose in distaste. "The bed has this nasty brown bedspread. I'm not touching it."

Her words reminded Jennie of what was missing here. She walked around a dividing wall that stuck partway out into the kitchen. Hidden behind the wall was a small mudroom leading to the back door, crammed with old boots and work shoes, shovels, rakes, tools, and a large garbage can. With relief, she noted the washer and dryer beneath precarious piles of newspapers. She prayed they worked.

They recognized the sound of Tim's footsteps and listened as he paused to peer into the rooms clustered close to the staircase. When he joined them in the kitchen, Jennie saw the familiar look in his eyes that said he was about to let his temper get the better of him. It was the expression that typically set his father off, which always resulted in the two of them fighting long and loud. She chose to ignore it whenever possible. She held up a hand as if to stop him.

"Don't, Tim, just don't. There's nothing you can say that we don't know."

"Can we go back home, please?" He made no effort to hide the fury behind his words. "Like, right now."

"You know there's no 'back home' to go to. This is home."

"No way. This is nobody's home. It should be torn down."

"Lucky for us it wasn't. This is about the best thing that's happened to us in a long time. So we're going to be grateful and make the best of it."

"I shouldn't have come." Tim gave his mother a defiant look. "Maybe I won't stay."

"And leave me here alone?" Willa was indignant. "Don't you dare."

Jennie was suddenly developing a headache. "Look, kids, it will be okay, really. We have a lot of work to do, but come on, it's not so bad. If we clean it up, paint, all that stuff, it'll be fine."

"But it's here," Willa moaned. "In this place. This weird, awful place."

"You don't know that it's weird or awful." Jennie massaged the bridge of her nose. "It could turn out to be great."

"This is not going to be a great place." Tim's voice rose. "Not now, not ever. And it's full of those creepy Amish people.

Come on, you saw the crazy buggies on the road. Those ugly black clothes—what's that about? And no electricity?"

Jennie had come to regret telling the children about the Amish people who populated the area. She'd thought it would be interesting to them, something they would enjoy learning about. Big mistake on her part, she realized; it had made them dread the move even more.

"That's part of their religion." Shep entered the room. Jennie noted that it only took the four of them standing there to make the kitchen feel crowded. "When you learn more about them, you might be a bit more tolerant. Your ignorance isn't their problem."

"Thanks for the lecture, Dad. You are so right. I'm the ignorant moron, not those people who think they're living in their own little world while everyone around them is in a different one."

"That's right. But don't worry, because they probably have no desire to spend any time with you."

Jennie could see it would take only a few more words to bring on a full-blown argument. When exactly had this started, she wondered, the two of them being unable to exchange more than three sentences without fighting, usually over nothing. What was happening now was stressful for the entire family. Stressful and constant. They could be talking about the weather, and the result would be the same.

It was hard to believe that Tim had once worshipped his father and that the two had spent every moment together when Shep came home from work at night. Just the sight of his little boy could always cheer him up, no matter how tough a day he'd had. He loved Willa, too, Jennie had never doubted that, but he'd always had a special connection with Tim.

Then rambunctious little Tim turned into a teenager with the bad combination of a nasty temper and a short fuse. It was toward his father that much of his anger was directed. Though none of them ever discussed it, Jennie knew the reason. She was hoping that the change in their circumstances would somehow bring about other changes, not just for Tim and Shep but for all of them. When things got difficult, Willa tended to retreat to her room, unreachable behind the walls she erected with her headphones or computer. She said and showed little about what she saw going on around her or how she felt about any of it. Tim acted up, and more often as time went on. His grades slipped, and his old friends started coming around less. Last November, he had been suspended from school for getting into a brawl in the hallway. Jennie wasn't sure how much more the threads holding the four of them together could take.

She turned to her husband. "Should we start unloading the car?"

He nodded. "I'll just go take a look at the upstairs first."

He left, and Jennie started to follow him out.

"Where are you going?" Willa asked.

"To help Dad unpack. I'd like your help, too. There's a lot to do." She looked over at her son. "Help from both of you."

He gave a loud sigh of irritation but moved to follow her. Smiling, she stretched out a hand to his shoulder, but he quickly and deliberately moved out of her reach. She tried not to show how much his reaction hurt her. Instead, she gave him a broad smile. "What do you say we bring in the cooler first, and I can set out some cold drinks and snacks for everyone. It'll help get our energy up!"

She hoped the note of hysteria creeping into her voice was only in her imagination. Her family was not going to fall apart. She would not allow it.

Chapter 2

Scrubbing the last remaining empty drawer in the kitchen, Jennie thought for the hundredth time that it had been a very long while since anyone had cleaned the insides of any drawer, closet, or cabinet in this house.

"I mean, *really*, people," she muttered, imitating Willa's teenage intonations. "*So* gross."

Finally deciding this was as good as it was going to get, she stood up and saw the sky growing light outside. After rinsing the rag she had used, she opened the back door far enough to hang it on the outside doorknob to dry, pausing to appreciate the quiet, mysterious moment as night transitioned into day. It had always been one of her favorite times when the children were small and she was the only one awake in the house, the family together, everything peaceful.

It's peaceful now, she couldn't help adding to herself, because they were all in tiny separate rooms, so they couldn't argue. She came back inside and knelt to pat Scout on the head. He had joined her in the kitchen when she had gotten out of bed an hour ago, only too glad to keep her company. She had been unable to sleep, consumed by all the things to wash and fix. Ever since they'd arrived eight days before, she had felt almost frantic, unable to decide what needed doing most. It was important to get the children's bedrooms set up so they would be settled in before school started. At the same time, she and Shep needed to get all the boxes unpacked and cleared out, and the kitchen had to be dealt with so the kids could have a welcoming place to eat or hang out. The entire house, it seemed, needed an overhaul. Yet her daily plans were always upended by some new problem, some roadblock that demanded her immediate attention. Not to mention such time-consuming necessities as registering the kids for school, filling out an ocean of forms, and scheduling appointments for everything from the cable company to the new pediatrician for school physicals. On mornings like these, she would attack a random small task that she knew she could complete, simply to have the satisfaction of seeing a task through to the end.

"Okay, Scout," she said, "that's one more thing cleaned and one more box about to be unpacked."

He yawned.

"You have very high expectations, you know that?"

In a corner, she found the carton marked *Kitchen—Odds and Ends,* and removed the items inside, everything from an old-fashioned eggbeater, chopsticks, and extra wooden spoons to an apple corer. As she was breaking down the box, she glanced at the old wall clock. Six-thirty already. How had that happened? She hastened upstairs to Tim, trying not to think about how tiny and dark his room was. It was an improvement over his prior sleeping arrangement back in Lawrence, the foldout couch in their living room. They'd had only two bedrooms in that house, so it was the best arrangement they could come up with. She had to believe that a dank little bedroom of his own was better than none. If only they could afford to paint, it would make such a difference. But that would have to wait.

"Honey, time to get up." She directed her words to the long lump beneath the sheet. No part of him was visible, his head hidden beneath the pillow.

She repeated herself more loudly.

"Nnnuuhhh . . ." The lump moved closer to the wall, trying to get away from the sound of her voice.

This had long been the usual morning procedure on a school day. She had to spend a good five minutes coaxing him awake. Even when he finally got out of the bed, he refused to look at her or speak, just stumbled past. She had given up on what he clearly considered outrageous demands, such as the idea that he should say good morning. From his room, she went next door to Willa's; her school bus came later, but she needed more time to get dressed than her brother. Waking up Willa was usually easier; she might even smile as she was coming to consciousness before recalling that she was no longer displaying affection to her parents if she could help it. Today, though, she remembered, as she gave her mother only a brief glare.

Jennie retreated to the kitchen, setting out bowls, spoons,

and a gallon of milk. Eventually, Tim appeared in jeans and a T-shirt, his hair uncombed. He said nothing, just yanked open the cabinet where he knew he would find cereal and slammed the box down on the table as he collapsed into a chair.

"Good morning."

He didn't respond to his mother's voice, only hunched down even farther as he poured cereal into a bowl.

"You'll take the bus home after school?"

He reached for the milk, shooting her a look that indicated the answer was obvious.

"Well, maybe there's a team or a club or something after school," she said. "Something that might interest you."

"Not only is there nothing in this stupid school that interests me, but I'd like to know how I could get home, since there's nobody to drive me." He began hurriedly gulping down big spoonfuls.

"Maybe ask someone . . ." Her voice trailed off. He was right, of course. He barely knew anyone at the school, and it would be tough to find someone willing to give him a ride. She was also forgetting that the houses were more spread apart around here than in Lawrence; there, it was easier to find someone who lived nearby.

She gave him an encouraging smile. "After today it'll be different. Dad'll have his truck, and I'll have the car all day, so I can get you."

"Oh, goody," he said, getting up and grabbing his books. "I can get my mommy to drive me around."

He stomped out of the room, and she heard the front door slam, hard. As if on cue, Willa entered the kitchen.

"What's his problem?" She slid into a chair, reaching for the cereal box. "Like there was ever a minute when he didn't have one."

Jennie stood there, watching Willa repeat the same procedure as her brother. Why was it, she wondered, that with her family, breakfast was always something to be endured rather than enjoyed.

"So what's on tap today at school?" Jennie asked in a hopeful voice.

Her daughter gave a mirthless laugh. "More boring classes, more boring kids. More boredom, basically."

"It will improve, you know. Please just give it some time and keep an open mind."

"'*Keep an open mind.*' Do you hear yourself?" She reached into her backpack and pulled out a brush, which she pulled through her long dark hair with one hand as she continued to eat with the other. "Mom, this school is the worst. You're making us go to this horrible place, so we are. Don't pretend it's going to be good. It's not." She stood, slung her backpack over one shoulder, and started out.

"Have a great day, honey. I love you," Jennie called to her retreating back.

A desultory wave was the reply.

She cleared the table. Shep was asleep, planning to get up at eight; he hadn't come home from the shop until after midnight. This morning they were going together to buy him a small used truck. He had been taking the car, unless she needed it. On those days, she would drop him off at the store and pick him up at the end of the day. They had known it would be impossible to exist here with one car and had decided it made more sense to get him something with room to transport bikes and other equipment if necessary. They hadn't expected to put off buying the truck for this long, but Howland's Bicycles and Repairs was taking up every minute that Shep didn't spend working on the house.

Jennie had yet to see the inside of the shop. He had allowed her to drop him outside, claiming he wanted to organize a bit first. From inside the car, she would try to peer into the store's darkened windows, hoping to see beyond the few bicycles there, but her attempts were useless. The windows needed cleaning, and there were boards of some kind behind the display bikes, blocking what was behind them. It all made her very nervous. She knew full well that being organized wasn't something her husband particularly cared about; it meant that he didn't want to upset her with the reality of whatever he had found there. Given Shep's sensitivity to his work problems over the years, however, she kept her fears to herself. Her goal, as she reminded herself numerous times a day, was to support his efforts at this endeavor. So far, all she knew was that he was utterly exhausted and in no way looked like an excited new business owner.

This kind of thinking won't lead anywhere good, she told

herself. She grabbed the dog's leash from a hook near the front door. "Come on, boy, let's go."

Scout was already by her side, barking and jumping up and down in excitement at the sight of the leash. They set off at a brisk pace in the warm September morning. Jennie had always taken Scout for a long morning walk. Here, they went to the end of the street and turned back onto the main road so they could go past the beautiful fields of the Amish farms. She enjoyed the peace of the cows and horses scattered about, the dogs and chickens, the occasional passing buggy.

"Could you live on a farm like these people?" she asked Scout, who trotted along beside her. "Nah, you're not really a farm kind of dog." She paused. "I *do* give you the benefit of the doubt, but you've never shown any interest."

As usual, she started out with the intention of walking fast enough to get her heart rate up, hoping it would help her shed those ten pounds she had been battling for as long as she could remember. Invariably, she would quickly get tired and give up on her resolution so she could enjoy the scenery. Now she slowed her pace, and Scout slowed as well.

"So, when are the kids going to settle into school?" she asked him. "I figured they wouldn't like it just on principle. Please tell me I'm right and they'll stop hating it at some point."

Silence.

"That's true—it's not as if I'm sending them to prison. These are perfectly nice schools. I only hope they find some friends. Even one friend each would be fine."

When the children had been little, she recalled, they'd had many friends, all those children in the neighborhood. She thought of them playing ball, riding bicycles along the narrow sidewalks. Tim had been born a year after she and Shep got married, and Willa two years after that, so, she calculated, she was remembering a time when Shep was probably done selling cars and had moved into selling insurance. They didn't have much money, but they were able to manage. Despite the seeds of doubt, there had been plenty of promise in her husband's career. How long had it taken them to realize that insurance wasn't going to work out for him, either?

It wasn't as if he hadn't worked hard at his jobs. He had. He was just ill suited to them. No one could blame him for that, considering they were practically handed to him after high school graduation. She thought about how eventful June of that year had been, the most exciting time of their life together. They had just gotten married and moved into a tiny one-bedroom apartment. Plus, everyone in town was only too happy to hire Shep Davis, hero of the school football team. He was the biggest deal to come along in many years. No job interviews or résumé writing for the star quarterback to bother with; local business owners made it clear they would welcome him with open arms. The job selling cars with Able Motors had seemed the most promising initially, with Leon Able arguing that, between his contacts and Shep's celebrity, the sky was the limit. She had been so proud of her handsome young husband that first week, wearing a new suit, sitting behind his own desk in the showroom, surrounded by shining cars. Success had seemed inevitable.

The problem was that no one had looked past his football-hero status to notice how shy he was around people he didn't know well. People loved coming in to meet him, talking about his winning seasons and dozens of game-changing plays. For the first year, it was as Leon Able said, and sales were strong. Then it seemed that everyone who wanted to buy a car from the local celebrity had done so. Customers who didn't know his story were polite when they saw the photos and awards Leon had prominently displayed, but that didn't mean they wanted to take the next step of plunking down thousands of dollars for a car. Shep didn't have any idea how to get them to take that next step, either. He did his best, but he was completely tongue-tied when it came to making small talk about anything other than football, and far too polite to push a product on someone.

Jennie had gotten pregnant with Tim only two months after their wedding, and any suggestion she made about getting a job herself was met with an instant refusal. There was no point, Shep insisted, because she needed to be at home with the baby. They were able to live on what he brought home for a few years, but the embarrassment of being the lowest producer in the showroom caught up with him. He changed companies, to get away from the disappointment in Leon Able's eyes. The result was the same at the next place.

At some point, he got the idea to sell insurance. He was fired up by the plan, convinced it was a product he would be more comfortable selling. He tried with three companies. His successes, which Jennie always fussed over and celebrated, were few and far between. When she tried to suggest he find a job in something other than sales, he would explode that he wasn't qualified to do anything at all, and he'd usually end up storming out of the house for several hours, getting as far away as he could from the argument and her pitying eyes.

Jennie once made the mistake of urging him to take the time to go to college. The look on his face made her drop the subject at once. His decision not to go to college was a subject he never talked about. He could have gone to any number of schools on a football scholarship, but he had been unwilling to leave his younger brother, Michael. Shep had been responsible for his brother ever since their mother died, when he was ten and Mike eight. Their father wasn't at home much, working the night shift as a waiter at a diner. He would leave for his shift at five in the afternoon and get back by five the next morning. That meant he would be asleep when the boys got up for school and gone by the time they got home from afterschool sports practices. Mostly, the two boys were alone. Shep took care of their meals, their laundry, and everything else a parent would have done. It wasn't that their father didn't love them. Losing his wife had left him broken inside, and it was only the desire to take care of his children that gave him a reason to get up and go to work every day. Unfortunately, the best job he could come up with was the one that kept him away from them most of the time. Shep would sometimes see him in the stands at his football games, still in his waiter's white shirt and black pants and shoes, looking tired but proud. When it came time to consider college, Shep wanted no part of leaving Michael home alone. He told Jennie that he was ready to marry her and get to work in the real world. College wasn't important anyway, he said. If he had any resentment over the fact that Michael went to college, then on to law school and a lucrative career, he never showed it.

Shep rarely showed his feelings on any subject to anyone but Jennie. They had met in high school; she had been shocked when the handsome eleventh-grade football star expressed an interest in her. He could have had almost any girl in the school at that point. She never could understand what he saw in her, the unpopular girl who was so quiet in classes. Later, she found out that he didn't like the parties or the fuss girls made over him, or the kids who just wanted to say they were pals with the best football player their school had ever produced. Jennie, he knew, didn't care. The two of them could sit and just be together. Plus, he was pleasantly surprised to discover she was far more outgoing away from school. "I always knew you weren't the quiet type," he'd said with a grin. "Don't know how I knew, but I just did."

He also loved the way she made him laugh. But she hadn't done that in a while, had she, she said to herself as she turned around to head home.

Of course, once they started dating, he quickly learned why she was so withdrawn at school. She didn't want to provide the other kids any more gossip about her than they already had. Despite the fact that she hadn't invited a single friend over to her house since elementary school, they somehow all knew about her parents. Knew that her father had rarely been around when she and her older sister, Hope, were little, and that he had finally disappeared altogether. Knew that her mother, Tess, was an alcoholic who once got by on whatever money her husband sent her, and when it stopped coming, she depended on the men she dated to cover her liquor and expenses. Hope and Jennie had seen a parade of men over the years, most of whom lasted fewer than six months. They didn't understand how their mother worked it out, but she always had enough money for their food and her alcohol, plus a new dress now and then. She was typically asleep during the day, so they would see her for a few hours in the early evening. That was Jennie's favorite part of the day, because her mother would start out sober, able to converse with them. Some days, she would be interested in chatting with Jennie about her day, or encouraging her to talk about her biggest dreams in life; she could be cheerful, even funny. Most days, though, she would complain bitterly about her husband and the rotten hand that life had dealt her. Either way, as the hours passed, she would drink more and get less lucid, finally waving Jennie away altogether. Eventually, she would fall asleep on the living room couch, the television on.

Jennie never stopped hoping that her mother would quit drinking one day, and they would be a happy family again, like when her father used to come home and stay for a week or two. Each visit started out the same way: her mother laughing and happy, singing in the kitchen and nicely dressed. Jennie was always certain that, this time, things were going to get better.

The problem was the way the visits ended. Sooner or later, Tess would start getting drunk again every evening. From her bed, Jennie could hear her parents arguing late into the night, Tess accusing her husband of having girlfriends on the road, and not caring about her or their children. Both of them yelled, and when they started throwing things, Jennie buried her head beneath her pillow. After a few days of this, he invariably left. What puzzled Jennie was that, if he actually did care for them as he claimed, why did he disappear for months on end, and then, finally, forever? Jennie's sister, Hope, told her she was a fool to think things would ever change, that their lives would stay miserable as long as they were there. Hope was furious at their mother for drinking and, as she saw it, driving their father away. She and Tess fought constantly. When Jennie was little, she would try to get in between them, hugging her mother's legs, crying and begging the two of them to stop shouting.

As Hope got older, the screaming matches usually led to her disappearing for long stretches, sometimes days at a time. The day she turned sixteen, she disappeared for good. After that, Tess retreated full-time to her bed. She lost all interest in how she and her remaining daughter would survive. Knowing her mother would only spend it on vodka, Jennie never told her about the cash she got in the mail every month, a hundred dollars, sometimes two hundred. She knew it was from Hope, although there was never a note or return address, just envelopes with postmarks from towns and cities all over the country, so many places that Jennie lost count. With that money and the income from after-school jobs, Jennie kept their tiny household afloat. She prayed Hope would come home, or at least allow Jennie to contact her, but neither ever happened. Equally upsetting was that she realized Hope was somehow getting news about them: The money stopped coming the month after Tess died of cancer, just before Jennie and Shep got married.

When Jennie started dating Shep, they discovered that they both lived without mothers, although for different reasons, and that they were the ones in charge at home. Slowly, they grew to trust each other. They viewed themselves as a team of two, needing no one else. At last, Jennie felt she had been right to believe in the possibility of a happy future. When they married and their son, Tim, was born, the overwhelming joy suddenly made it clear to Jennie why her mother had named her own first child Hope. It was the first time Jennie could understand how brutal the loss of a young mother's dream of a happy family must have been. Unfortunately, it was too late to share any of that with Tess.

They were genuinely happy for the first half of their marriage. It wasn't until later, when the endless money worries had worn them both down, that things began to change. Shep was stung by his self-described failure to provide for them. He stopped talking to her about work altogether. Several years ago, he had started taking jobs as a handyman, doing whatever he could find, to supplement his small income. Still, he refused to let Jennie get a job, and the more she pushed the issue, the more he withdrew from her. It was infuriating, even though she understood it was a matter of pride for him that his wife not work. She could see the damage already done to his ego by his dwindling paychecks. She decided to let the matter drop. Putting up with the financial hardship, she decided, was preferable to finding that she had lost all connection to him.

It didn't help. The cramped house and strained monthly budget took their toll. Her good-natured husband grew increasingly irritable. His problems with Tim escalated as their son got older, and he spent precious little time with Willa. Worst of all to Jennie was the slow upward creep in the number of beers he drank on the weekends, and then on the weekdays as well. The idea that he might become an alcoholic struck terror into her heart. She had always worried that she'd inherited her mother's tendencies, so she never touched alcohol herself. She was vigilant about warning her son of his possible legacy, trying—although she wondered how successfully—to keep him away from situations where he might be offered alcohol. Soon, she knew, she would have to start talking to Willa about it as well. The idea that her husband could fall into the trap was something that had never occurred to her. His retreat into periodic alcohol-induced numbness was obvious to the children, and it fueled Tim's anger and Willa's overall sadness.

This move was supposed to be their fresh start, the chance to start over. So why didn't it feel that way?

Approaching the house, she unclipped Scout's leash from his collar and let him bound ahead to the front door. Shep was sitting at the kitchen table, drinking coffee.

"Morning." He gave her a tired smile.

"Ready to go truck shopping?"

"Soon as I finish this, I guess."

She poured herself some coffee and sat across the table from him. "Maybe after, you'll take me to see inside the shop."

He refused to meet her eyes. "Maybe."

She knew what that meant, but she gave him the brightest smile she could muster. "I've got a feeling about this day, you know? I can tell it's going to be a good one."

Chapter 3

"Lovely day," Jennie called out.

Now that she had established a regular walking routine with Scout, she had been passing by this house at the same time every morning for several weeks. Each time she had seen the same Amish woman sweeping the steps leading from an enclosed front porch. It was a setting suitable for a painting. The house was white with green shutters, set in front of a barn and several other buildings. It appeared as if several additions had been built onto the house over time. The porch had rocking chairs and hanging plants, an appealing spot to relax, she thought. A gray-topped buggy sat outside the barn, as if waiting for a horse to bring it to life.

After the first several weeks of Jennie's walks, she and the woman had started exchanging waves. Today she was venturing further, not knowing whether her words would be considered neighborly or an intrusion.

"Yes, it is." The woman paused and smiled. "You and your dog enjoy a morning walk together, yes?"

Jennie was delighted by the friendly response. She knew virtually nothing about the Amish and was fearful of stepping over some invisible line that everyone else knew not to cross. Apparently, it was all right to converse with them, uninvited. She had seen them in town, shopping in food stores and other places, so she understood that they didn't keep completely to themselves, but this was her first proof that they didn't mind talking to outsiders—the *English,* as she now knew they were called. Or at least this particular woman didn't mind.

"My favorite part of the day," Jennie called out, realizing it was true.

The woman nodded and resumed her task. Jennie felt entitled by this exchange to steal an extra moment to stare at her crisp white bonnet, with its untied strings hanging down, and her dark purple dress beneath a black apron. Despite the light chill in the October air, the woman was barefoot. She finished sweeping and went back inside, leaving Jennie to admire the pristine grounds visible from her vantage point near the road. Like Mary Poppins, *practically perfect.* She smiled, recalling the phrase from the book, one of her childhood favorites that she had read to her children when they were small. She wondered how many hours this woman spent maintaining the yard, with its neatly bordered flower beds and healthy carpet of lawn. There were many nice yards in the area, but every one she could identify as Amish was exactly as neat as this one. She and Shep had put in what seemed like a thousand hours on theirs, and it didn't look half as good. It probably takes several years, she reassured herself, to get it to this state.

"In our case, several decades," she muttered.

Passing by on her return about twenty minutes later, she was surprised to see the same Amish woman emerge from her house, drying her hands on a dish towel. "I see your dog is limp-ing. Can I help you?" she asked.

Startled, Jennie looked at Scout to see that he was indeed limping, trying to avoid putting weight on his right front leg. The woman must have noticed it from her window as she watched them approach.

"Oh, my. He must have stepped on something."

The woman held open the door for her guest. "We have a dog, too. We don't allow him in the kitchen, but this is a spe-cial situation. Please bring him in."

Nodding her thanks, Jennie came up the path and got a closer look at her neighbor. She was very pleasant-looking, blue-eyed, with a high forehead and full mouth. No makeup, no jewelry. Her age was difficult to gauge, but Jennie guessed between forty and fifty. Pulled-back blond hair peeked out from beneath her white head covering, the side pieces appearing to be braided but, on closer inspection, turning out to be tightly twisted.

Jennie stepped into a large combination kitchen–family room, lit by daylight peeking beneath dark green blinds on the windows. There wasn't much furniture, but everything was im-maculate. A dark wood cabinet contained fine china, visible through its double glass doors. The focal point of the room was a large wooden table with a bench on either side and a chair at each end. Off to one side, Jennie noted a sofa and two rocking chairs. There was also a small table over in one corner with art supplies and a low bookshelf beside it containing children's books. On the floor nearby was a wooden dollhouse. The only decorations on the walls were a calendar and a clock, no photographs or paintings anywhere. The kitchen area looked similar to any other kitchen, as far as she could make out. No overhead lighting fixtures but a refrigerator. She was confused, knowing the Amish stayed away from electricity. How could they have a refrigerator? There was a lamp atop a small side table as well. Large bowls of fruits, vegetables, and other ingredients for a meal covered nearly all the counter space. From where she stood, she could identify potatoes, zucchini, apples, and glass jars with noodles and what was probably flour. With so much food arrayed, she guessed they must be getting ready for company.

She realized she was staring and recovered enough to introduce herself, extending a hand. "I'm Jennie Davis. My family moved into—" She started to gesture.

"Bert Howland's house." The woman smiled. "A new neighbor is news that people are quick to share. My name is Mattie Fisher. Welcome."

They both knelt to examine Scout's paw, locating the sore spot and extracting a thorn. Mattie washed his paw with a wet dish towel.

"Poor thing," Jennie said to him.

"He will be all better now," Mattie said. She went over to

the table and picked up a plate of cookies, extending them to her guest. "Chocolate chip, baked this morning."

As the plate of cookies was extended, a recovered Scout took a confident step forward to as if to make his selection.

"No," Jennie told him. "Not for you." She looked up apologetically. "I've let him believe he's the boss, I'm afraid."

Mattie laughed. "They are quick to take the job, aren't they? Please sit down."

Jennie was entranced by the woman's lilting accent. She took the proffered chair and got Scout to sit close to her feet.

"I see you have children."

"Eight. The oldest is sixteen, and my little Moses is four."

Jennie's eyes opened wide. Eight kids, and the house was as clean as a hospital operating room. "I only have two, but I can't say my house is as . . . organized as this. We've been busy fixing it up, though."

The other woman nodded. "We knew Bert Howland for many years. His wife died a long time ago. It is difficult to be alone with the business and the house. I guess it needs some work, yes?"

"*Some* work, no. *Much* work. But that's fine. We'll do it one thing at a time, as we can."

"That is surely the way." Mattie nodded. "With patience, yes?"

Jennie bit into a cookie, thinking that she liked this woman very much. Despite their obvious differences, she felt comfortable talking to her. And boy, she thought, could she ever bake; the cookie was delicious.

"Do you mind if I ask what kind of farm this is? I don't know much about farming, so please excuse my ignorance."

"It is a dairy farm. There are forty cows in the barn, and we grow crops to feed them. My husband, Abraham, is in the fields now with my oldest son, Peter."

"Where are the other children? In school?"

"Most of them. My older daughter and my youngest are at my sister's, helping out with her children this morning. They'll be back anytime now, so we can get dinner ready. We eat at eleven-thirty."

"All that food is just for dinner?"

Mattie smiled. "Not all. Some things we will get started for supper later. That is when everyone eats together. And your children?"

Jennie talked a bit about Tim and Willa, and Mattie asked how they liked their new schools. She answered as diplomatically as she could, not wanting to lie but having no desire to explain the disaster the school year had been so far. Then, guessing her hostess needed to get back to her tasks, she thanked her warmly and took Scout to the door.

"I will see you again, yes?" Mattie said. "Probably if you walk by tomorrow."

"Yes. I'll look forward to it."

As Jennie and Scout reached the road, she turned back to wave, but Mattie was already gone. There was a serenity about the woman that was striking, she thought. No sense of being rushed, having a million things on her mind—the hallmarks of virtually everyone she knew. Eight kids, yet Mattie had time to practically sterilize her home and bake cookies. Maybe she was put here just to make me feel guilty, Jennie mused, smiling. The woman's questions hadn't been prying, but straightforward, asked with genuine interest. Jennie was already looking forward to her walk tomorrow, hoping she would see Mattie again.

As she drew close to her house, she spotted Shep getting into their truck. He saw her and paused to wave. Today was the day he was finally taking her to see the store.

She jogged over to him. "Were you leaving without me?" she asked.

"No, of course not." He smiled. "I wouldn't sneak off. Just thought I'd wait in the truck, go over some papers."

"Okay, hang on a sec."

Putting the dog in the house, she practically flew to get into her car before Shep pulled away. It wasn't that she didn't know the way to the store, but if she let him go without her, she wasn't sure when he would next agree to let her see the place. It had been over a month already, and she had waited patiently for this day. More than patiently, in her opinion. At long last, she would find out what the big mystery was.

He pulled out of the driveway, and she followed. Nervously, she parked her car next to his truck in the small lot and waited while he unlocked the store's front door. They went inside, small bells above the door tinkling to indicate someone had entered. "Quaint," she remarked of the sound.

Shep hastened to the back to turn on fluorescent lights. The space wasn't huge, but it was more than adequate. That, she realized, was pretty much the only positive thing she could come up with. Her impression was that it was dark and dingy, and whether it was in truth or not, it felt dusty and dirty. The air was stale, smelling of rubber. The walls were a dreary olive green, the floor a nondescript speckled linoleum. There was a long, narrow passageway running the length of the store, the only place to walk, formed by bicycles crowded along both sides. She went toward a counter in the back beneath a small *Repairs* sign that must have been thirty years old. Numerous newspaper articles and flyers were messily tacked up on a bulletin board. The large cash register was so old, she noted, it was probably considered vintage. That was the one thing that might qualify as having a touch of charm, she reflected; everything else looked original in a way that desperately needed replacing. She went behind the counter, opening the door to the back room, where repairs were done. It was a dark mess, tools and bicycle parts strewn about. A bare lightbulb and the sunlight fighting its way through a small, grimy window provided the only illumination.

Shep came to stand behind her. "So this is my palace." He put his hands on her shoulders.

She turned to look at him, not sure what to say. If this was the result of a month's hard work, she supposed she should be grateful he hadn't brought her here before. It wasn't that the place was terrible, but it was not a store you'd want to be in for any longer than necessary. Old, dreary, tired—she could have gone on, but what was the point? The house had been disappointing as well, but only the four of them had to be in it. This was a place of business, supposed to attract paying customers, and it was downright depressing. Glancing over at the many bicycles crammed together, she wondered how a customer could even get one out to look at it. Maybe Bert Howland had a strong following based on his years in the area, but unless those people were legally bound to keep coming here, she and Shep were in trouble. It was going to be mighty difficult to support their family if their entire income came from fixing the occasional flat tire.

"You've probably done a huge amount of work, getting this place into shape."

He nodded. "You wouldn't have believed what it was like."

"Do any customers come in?" She tried to keep her voice light.

"Not many. Most of them just see that the store is open again and want to know who took over for Bert. Been a few repairs, nothing big. That's okay, though, because it's given me time to study this stuff."

"Right." She had seen him carrying manuals in and out of the house, teaching himself bicycle repairs.

"I've been taking apart different types of bikes and putting them back together. No problem. I got this."

"That's great, honey." She meant it, although she knew he would be quick to pick up the business of repairs; there was very little he couldn't fix. "Is there some inventory list somewhere, someplace he kept track of all these bikes?"

"Haven't found one yet. That's something I gotta do soon." He shook his head. "This guy kept bad records. Or none at all."

"I'm guessing no computer."

"You guessed correctly, madam."

"So you need one here."

He shrugged. "Need a lot of stuff here. Can't afford any of it, so we'll make do."

She gazed at him, feeling a mix of sympathy and admiration for the way he refused to complain. "You could use some help here, honey," she said. "I'm around, and I could—"

His face turned hard. "No. This is my store, and I'll handle this end of things. You have the house to deal with, and you're doing a great job with it. Plus the kids. They need you home after school, not working here with me."

"It doesn't have to be full-time. I—"

"No."

She couldn't believe it. The same old stubbornness on this subject. She took a step back, and his arms dropped to his sides.

"How long can you keep refusing to see that we *need* me to work?"

"We don't. When that day comes, I'll let you know."

She stared at him, her anger building. "It's ridiculous."

His expression turned sorrowful. "Sweetheart, can't you see that I have to do this myself? If I can't make it work, there's nothing else left to try."

Once again, she was torn between wanting to let him find his own way and resenting what he was putting the rest of them through because of his pride. Exasperated, she turned to leave. When she reached the door and yanked it open, she found the tinkle of the bells incredibly annoying.

Chapter 4

The house's walls were too thin to prevent Willa's crying from being heard in the hallway. Jennie stopped outside her daughter's bedroom door, listening, then gave a tentative knock.

"Sweetie, can I come in?"

A muffled answer. "Go away."

"Come on, Willa. You know I won't go away, so let me come in now. Please."

Silence. Though none of the bedroom doors had locks, Jennie would have preferred Willa to give her permission to enter.

"I'm opening the door now, okay?"

Her daughter was lying on the bed, staring at the ceiling, her face wet and red. This was not a good day for either of her children, Jennie thought. She, Shep, and Tim had just returned from a school football game, where Tim once more sat on the bench the entire time. Despite attending all the practices, he had yet to play in a single game this season. He had numerous, bitterly explained reasons: The coach didn't like him, he had missed precious training time before they moved here, he wasn't a real part of the team because he was the new kid. Whatever the reason, he claimed his high school football career was over; he would never get anywhere after sitting out the season.

Jennie's heart broke for him. He had always known he would never be the football star his father was, but he enjoyed playing and had shown some promise the previous year. It was also one of the few interests he and Shep had in common. Over the past few years, they would sit together every so often to watch a game on a fall Saturday, forgetting to argue as they alternately cheered and yelled at the television. Not being allowed to play made Tim hate his new school even more. Jennie understood that he had been counting on football as a way to get included in the social scene and a way to make himself known, and that path was being blocked off. The ride home today had been grim, their son silently staring out the window. Shep had closed the store for an hour to catch the end of the game, and asked Tim if he would come back to help with the inventory Shep was finally doing, but Tim just glared and shook his head. Both Shep and Jennie had been angered by his flat refusal, telling him he had to do his part to make the family's move succeed. The ensuing argument resulted in Shep speeding out of the driveway alone, brakes screeching, and Tim retreating to his bedroom, slamming the door behind him.

Now it was Willa's turn to be miserable.

Jennie sat down on the bed and stroked her daughter's shoulder. "What's wrong?"

"Nothing. Everything." Willa rolled away to lie facedown.

"Okay. Let's start with one thing."

The girl held up her head to look at her mother. "Mr. Bradley hates me. I'm going to fail English."

"Why do you think that? Has there been a test or—"

"And nobody likes me." The words seemed to burst out of her. "I don't have a single friend here. Everybody thinks I'm a total loser. Which I am!"

"Oh, no, honey, that's not true at all. You're the furthest thing from a loser."

"Mom, you don't know what you're talking about."

"You're a little shy, so it takes some time for kids to get to know you, that's all."

The girl groaned in exasperation. "Could you please just stop? Just stop. And leave."

She put her face down and folded her arms to cover her head as if she couldn't tolerate the sight of her mother. Jennie sat there for a few moments, then left the room. The truth was, she was at a loss as to how to advise her child. She didn't know what the kids here were like, what the school was like, or even what Willa was like with other kids. She felt useless.

Nothing seemed to be going well for any of them. It was clear that the store wasn't doing well, and Shep's early hopefulness was ebbing. Both the children were unhappy. She was spending her days sanding, patching, and repairing throughout the house, unable to afford to do things right, and feeling as if she were holding the place together with glue and bobby pins. Every afternoon she began the long process of comforting her children as they returned home from another bad day at school. First she would greet a long-faced Willa as she got off the bus and dragged herself to the front door. Jennie had been warned by her daughter not to dream of going out to meet the bus, where the other kids could see her, so she would stay in the kitchen, usually setting out a glass of milk and some cookies, as if this time-honored tradition would somehow help. Her daughter might sip at the milk and take a bite or two of a cookie, all the while reciting a litany of wrongs, injustices, and complaints. Jennie would do her best, but reassurances and advice seemed futile at best. Later, she would leave to pick up Tim from practice. The process was pretty much the same, although he typically ate five or so cookies while he complained. The three of them would have dinner at six-thirty, as Jennie kept up what felt like mindless chatter, while the children alternated between silence and irritability. Then they would retreat to their rooms, theoretically to do homework. Shep usually got home around eight o'clock. *Rinse and repeat*, she thought. This time there were no cookies, and the milk was replaced by a beer. She would serve Shep dinner and sit with him, but he would be nearly as silent as the children. At least, she reflected, he wasn't irritable. Again, the only thing she could think of was to keep up a distracting stream of chatter about what she had seen or done that day. Not exactly gripping stuff, she thought.

She had been so happy when they were about to move here and he had opened up about his hopes for the new business he was about to inherit, how he would make things work out for sure this time. It had been so long since he had confided in her that way. It was a big part of what had convinced her that this was really going to be their fresh start. Once it became clear that life here wasn't going to go the way he'd imagined, the old walls came back up. He was locked deep inside himself and wasn't letting her in. She was at a loss. Should she beg him to talk to her? Demand it? She didn't know how long they could go on with him being the only one who knew exactly how much financial trouble they were in, and refusing her help on any level.

She wished there were someone who wanted to feed *her* milk and cookies and listen to her complain for a while.

It was quiet now, and she had a couple of hours before she had to start dinner. She grabbed a light jacket and left the house. She had to get some air, find something other than the sense of failure that clung to her as she cleaned or cooked in that broken-down kitchen. Without even thinking about it, she turned at the corner toward the Fisher house. Since the day several weeks back when Mattie had invited her in for coffee, the two of them had exchanged greetings and sometimes stopped to chat when Jennie took her morning walks. She found her encounters with the Amish woman invariably soothing and would go on her way cheered and optimistic. Whatever quality it was that Mattie possessed, Jennie wished she had it as well. Patience, or maybe acceptance. Perhaps it was a sense of security about who she was, or a feeling that her life was what it was supposed to be. Jennie couldn't put her finger on it. All she knew was that she could use some of it right now, and she was about to find out if a surprise visit was another thing considered acceptable by the Amish.

Up until today, Jennie hadn't encountered anyone besides Mattie when she went by the house. Surprised to see children in Amish dress outside, she recalled that today was Saturday, so of course the schedule would be different. Three children were crouching down by a flower bed, examining something, their heads close together. A teenage girl was walking toward the house, holding the hand of a little boy who looked to be around five or six. Two men wearing wide-brimmed straw hats stood outside the barn, talking. From this distance, she guessed one was Mattie's husband, Abraham. The other might be their eldest son, Peter. She stopped, taking in the scene before her, a busy family engaged in activities. Compare this with her family, she reflected, isolated from one another, all sulking in different places. She closed her eyes, overcome by sadness.

She heard her name being called and opened her eyes to see Mattie on the front steps, smiling.

"A nice surprise. Please come and meet my family." Mattie waved her over and met Jennie halfway, leading her to the flower bed. The children stood up as their mother and her guest approached.

"This is Mrs. Davis." Mattie pointed to the children as she said their names, starting with the oldest. "Joshua, Becky, and Aaron."

Jennie thought she had never seen such adorable, well-mannered children. As they were introduced, they looked her directly in the eyes with some obvious curiosity, smiled politely, and nodded. The boys wore dark pants with suspenders and dark blue short-sleeved shirts. Their blond hair showed beneath straw hats with flat brims and a black band, smaller versions of what their father wore. Becky, like the other girl Jennie had seen walking to the house, wore a replica of what her mother had on, a white head covering and a long dress, minus the apron. The girl had the same pulled-back hairstyle, down to the neatly twisted side pieces.

"I'm glad to meet you," Jennie said. "I live nearby, so we're neighbors. Well, in the same neighborhood."

"Do you live on a farm?" Joshua asked. He had an accent like his mother's, Jennie noted.

"No, not a farm. Just a house. My husband runs a bicycle shop."

The little girl's eyes lit up. "We know how to ride tricycles. Do you want to see?"

Mattie frowned. "We do not put on such shows."

Becky turned at once to her mother, looking abashed.

Jennie didn't understand what had just transpired but sensed she had somehow caused the discord. "Perhaps I'll come by one day when you're on your tricycle, and I'll see you riding."

They were interrupted by the arrival of Mattie's husband and the boy, who did turn out to be their oldest son, Peter. Further introductions were made. Abraham had a beard but no mustache, and his hair was in the long bowl cut Jennie had seen on other Amish men, with bangs across the fore-head.

"You and your family are in Bert Howland's house, yes? My wife tells me you walk here with your dog. You didn't bring him today?" Abraham asked, setting down several empty buckets.

In her haste to get away, Jennie realized she hadn't thought to bring Scout. "No, but he would be delighted to come by anytime. He loves meeting new people."

Abraham let out a piercing whistle, and from behind the barn, a large dark brown dog appeared, racing across the grass until he reached them. Abraham made a clicking sound, and the dog immediately sat down, panting but otherwise immo-bile. "This is Hunter."

Jennie laughed. "I can't imagine my dog being half as obedi-ent as that. He would no more come when I whistled or sit like that than he would fly to the moon."

"He spends time with me, and I teach him. It's not hard," Abraham said with a smile.

"Can you teach me to do that with my children?" Jennie said it without thinking, then froze, afraid she had gone too far.

Both Mattie and Abraham laughed. "If only it were that easy, yes?" Mattie said.

Relieved, Jennie turned to Peter, who had been standing quietly. He was tall, and slightly darker than his parents in skin tone and hair, but his eyes were identical to his mother's.

"Do you work with your father on the farm after school?" she asked.

"I'm finished with school." His words held no trace of his

parents' accents. "We're done in our regular school after eighth grade. Then we have some regular meetings until we're fourteen, but it's more about our work and what we do with our time. I'm sixteen. And yes, I help on the farm."

"One day this will be his farm, and I will help him," Abraham added.

Peter didn't say anything, and Jennie wondered if she saw something in his eyes that didn't look happy. She admonished herself to stop reading into things about which she knew nothing.

"Well, I don't mean to interrupt your day. I just wanted some fresh air, really."

"I am about to go into the vegetable garden. If you have time, I will show it to you," Mattie said.

Jennie brightened. "I'd love that. Maybe I could learn how to plant a few vegetables myself. I've always wanted to."

She said good-bye to the men. As they turned away, she heard Abraham say something to his son in another language, and Peter responded in kind.

"Does your family normally speak in"—she hesitated—"is it German?"

"It is our language, called Pennsylvania Dutch. You would say a dialect of German. Our Bible and songbook are in German, though."

"And you all speak English as well. Wow."

She followed Mattie around to the back of the house. They passed another large white barn, and Jennie saw through its open doors that it was, for the most part, dedicated to the horses, with multiple stalls and a wide-open area where two horses were nuzzling; a walled-off section acted as a garage for two closed buggies and a smaller, open one.

When they reached the garden, Jennie's eyes widened. "This is huge. Do you do all this yourself?"

"My older daughter, Sarah, and the little ones help."

"What are you growing?"

They walked up and down the neat rows, Mattie pointing as she spoke. "Many things are done for the season, and the garden is cleaned out. Over there are lettuce and string beans. We grow many herbs. Here we have parsley, dill, mint, and some watercress. Here is where we had cucumbers, tomatoes, and squash. Oh yes, peas and eggplant. We grow about twenty-five different things."

"It's beautiful. I'd love to watch when you plant something, maybe learn how to do it."

Mattie smiled. "I would be very glad to show you."

Jennie looked around at the barn and fields beyond. "It's so lovely here. Peaceful."

"Thank you."

"I wish . . ." Jennie fell silent. Mattie looked at her, kindness in her eyes, but said nothing. "Time to get going." Jennie straightened up as if bracing for the return home. "I'm so glad I got to see your family."

"This was just a few of them. You must meet the rest. They are busy with chores. We do a lot of cleaning on Saturday because tomorrow we go to worship."

Jennie nodded as they went toward the road. "I can fit all of my family into one quick introduction. But I hope you'll meet them soon."

"It will be good to have a chance."

They reached the front of the house, exchanging good-byes before Mattie went inside. Feeling buoyed by the visit, Jennie was determined to go home and turn things around somehow. Could she get the kids to play a board game? She would make popcorn or drive somewhere to pick up ice cream. They weren't little anymore, but surely they could come up with something to do that didn't involve sitting in front of the television or a computer screen. All she knew was that this was going to be a fun-filled Saturday night at her house if it killed her.

Chapter 5

The market was busy on this Saturday morning, but far less than it would be in the warmer months, when crowds of tourists came to shop. Jennie meandered up and down the wide aisles, enjoying the sights and colors of the virtual sea of homemade and local goods. She loved the sheer variety of things for sale, from candles, quilts, and baskets to meats, herbs, and funnel cakes. At some point she hoped to be able to buy one of the Amish-made glider rocking chairs. She spent at least twenty minutes examining a selection of preserves and pickled foods, finally deciding to buy sauerkraut to serve with hot dogs later in the week. After paying, she realized she was right near one of her favorite booths and veered in another direction, hoping to resist the lure of fudge and soft pretzels. Getting down to the reason she had come today, she stopped to select potatoes and other ingredients to make a salad for supper.

Some of the vendors behind the stalls were Amish, but many were not. Everyone was friendly, and shopping here made for a much more personal and entertaining experience than at the huge supermarket. This was one aspect of their life in Pennsylvania that was special—having this unusual old marketplace right nearby. Unfortunately, she was the only one in her family who cared. Shep was too consumed with the store even to come by, and when she had dragged the kids with her one Saturday, they had busied themselves on their cell phones and shown no interest at all

On the way to the exit, Jennie passed some wooden mailboxes for sale and thought how nice it would be to replace the old one in front of their house. She had to smile, thinking how very far down on the list that item would fall.

The beautiful weather on the drive home was a welcome distraction from her thoughts, an unusually warm November day allowing her to open the car window and enjoy a pleasant breeze. As she approached the turn onto her street, she was surprised to see her husband and children standing by the side of the road with Abraham Fisher and his son Peter. Shep's truck was parked, and they were all gathered by the Fishers' buggy, Willa petting the horse as the men talked, their sons standing a little way off, engrossed in their own conversation. As far as Jennie knew, Shep had never met the Fishers, so she wondered what had brought about this little conference. The cars behind her made her less inclined to stop and interfere, so she drove past with a honk and a wave but saw in the rearview mirror that only Willa looked up. She wondered if the Fishers had tourists honking at them frequently so had learned to tune it out.

She greeted an excited Scout when she got home, then washed and cut up the newly purchased vegetables. When the rest of her family still hadn't returned, she reached for her cell phone to text Willa. Shep wasn't a fan of the cell phone; he always forgot to check his texts and kept his phone on silent, so she rarely bothered to attempt communicating with him that way. Her children never answered a call from her, and Tim, she knew, was likely to ignore any text from her as well. Her daughter was the only one who might bother to reply.

Where are you guys? she typed.

Fisher farm, came back the answer.

Apparently, the roadside chat had turned into something more. Jennie was thrilled that Shep might be getting to know Abraham Fisher a bit. That also probably meant her kids were meeting some of Mattie's children. Tim had shown only disdain toward the Amish so far. She hoped spending a little time with them would show him how wrong he was to judge people that way. Maybe some of their good manners would rub off on him. She almost laughed out loud at the image of her son sweetly obeying because he had seen an Amish child do it.

"If only . . ." she murmured.

Deciding she couldn't bear to be left out of the action, she beckoned to Scout to join her, and they set out on foot for the farm. Sure enough, there was Shep's red truck parked in front. On the far side of the house, she saw Tim and Peter sitting on the ground, talking comfortably. Fantastic, she thought. She hoped it was all right for Mattie's boy to have a non-Amish friend; it certainly made her happy to think her son might befriend him. A good influence, for a change.

She caught a glimpse of her husband crossing the open doorway to the barn. When she reached it, she found herself at the end of two long rows of enormous black-and-white cows, all facing away from one another. The smell of the animals was strong, but the barn was noticeably clean. The two men were halfway down the aisle, Abraham pointing out something while Shep studied one of the cows with great intensity.

"Hi there," she called softly, afraid of scaring the cows. That brought no response, and she realized how silly it was to imagine that her voice had the power to scare these massive animals. She called out again, louder.

Both men looked up. Shep smiled and gestured for her to come over. "Abraham is showing me around," he said to her. "Look at this system they have for collecting the milk."

As he explained and gestured, she was struck by how relaxed his face looked, more relaxed than she had seen him since, well, since they'd moved here. He was clearly so engaged by what they were discussing that his problems were momentarily forgotten. Silently, she thanked Abraham for doing what she had been unable to do.

"I saw you all together on the road before. How did that occur?" she asked Shep.

"Turns out Tim knows Peter. They waved, so I wound up stopping, and we all just started to talk."

A girl of around ten appeared in the doorway, one of the younger daughters, Jennie surmised, and informed her father that dinner was ready. He nodded.

"My Emma," he informed the Davises as she turned to leave. "You must stay and have dinner with us." Jennie and Shep protested, but Abraham ignored them. He called out after his daughter. "Our four guests will eat with us."

"Yes, Papa." She disappeared.

Jennie felt terrible about inflicting her entire family on Mattie with no warning, but there was nothing to be done. On the other hand, she was curious about having a meal with an Amish family. The three of them went to the house, the boys getting up and brushing themselves off when they saw their parents approach. Willa, it turned out, was already in the kitchen, standing off to one side while the younger children were busy setting out dishes and platters of cold food.

Mattie gave Jennie a big smile. "You are all here at last."

Names were exchanged. After Peter, there were three girls, Sarah, Nan, and Emma, the little girl who had come to the barn. Jennie hoped her own daughter was noting that the older two were fifteen and thirteen, surely potential friends for her. They were followed by eight-year-old Joshua, six-year-old Becky, and the two youngest boys. Though Jennie recalled meeting some of them earlier, every child stood politely and offered a greeting. Tim and Willa, she noted, had the good grace not to sulk, though she wouldn't have described their attitudes as enthusiastic. Shep, on the other hand, warmed up to

Mattie and the children immediately, seeming uncharacteristically comfortable with the novelty of this large family gathering for a midday meal.

The Fishers found their seats, one parent at either head of the table. Willa and Tim sat down together, but Willa jumped up when she realized she was sitting on the boys' side. Her face turned bright red. Jennie wanted to hug her and tell her it wasn't a big deal but knew that would only intensify her daughter's embarrassment.

Abraham announced they would say a silent grace, after which Mattie and the girls got up to serve the hot food. Jennie tried to help, but Abraham gestured for her to remain seated. She surveyed what was already arrayed before her: applesauce, bread and butter, beet salad, coleslaw, and two large pitchers of lemonade. Steaming platters of chicken and noodles were set down along with huge bowls of broccoli and squash. She considered what it would be like cooking meals for ten people three times every day. With the addition of the Davis family, Mattie was serving fourteen today, but she appeared as placid as always. Once you were dealing with ten, Jennie thought, throwing in a few more probably didn't matter much. She suspected that Mattie could have thrown in a few dozen more without being fazed.

Abraham and Shep discussed carpentry while the others ate, their silence punctuated only by requests to pass this or that. Clearly, Jennie noted, Abraham was the boss around this household. The children did not interrupt, much less ask questions or offer opinions on any subject. How different from their table, she thought, with her two children voicing their usually dissenting opinions whenever the mood seized them, and expecting their parents' full attention when they did so. Right now Tim looked impatient, while Willa kept her eyes down for most of the meal. Jennie took the opportunity to look more closely at the Fisher children, all remarkably neat in the middle of the day in their jewel-toned dresses or shirts and black pants. Even the four-year-old was managing his meal, his siblings assisting him when necessary. Jennie was sitting across from Tim, and when she felt the familiar sensation of her son nervously jiggling his leg, she shot him a dark look, and he stopped.

"Everything is delicious," she said. "Did any of it come from your garden?"

Mattie looked out over the table. "The beets, the cabbage and carrots in the coleslaw. The vegetables. Oh, and we grow the apples that I used for the applesauce."

"Fantastic," Jennie said.

"But we did not," Mattie added in a teasing tone, "grow the chocolate for the chocolate cake or the coffee beans for the coffee."

"We are too lazy," Abraham put in with a smile.

Shep and Jennie laughed. Mattie and her daughters commenced clearing the dishes and brought out dessert. Again, the boys made no move to assist, so Jennie held back from directing Tim to clear his own dishes; it wasn't appropriate for her to impose her views on these people. She noted that he and Peter were talking quietly. She thought it odd that her son had never mentioned meeting Peter, but then again, he rarely mentioned anything that went on in his life.

As the rich-looking chocolate cake was being cut, Abraham and Shep agreed that they would work together after the meal to repair some broken fencing by the chicken house. In exchange, Abraham would show Shep how he had repaired the roof when it was damaged in a storm. Her husband hadn't forgotten their roof was going to need work, Jennie realized. It was just another problem he was carrying around in his head, not discussing with her.

"Are you all right?"

Mattie's concerned question made Jennie realize she had sighed aloud.

She smiled. "Of course. Better than all right. I love this cake, which I should definitely not be eating."

"A little sweetness is nice, yes?"

"Always," she agreed.

As everyone got up after the meal, Tim came around the table to his mother. "Peter and I are going to hang out for a while," he informed her.

"Why didn't you tell me you knew him?" she asked, smiling. "That's so great. How did you meet?"

Tim shrugged. "Around. So I'll see you later."

"Where are you two going?"

Tim either didn't hear or chose to ignore her. She watched him and Peter lope off together as Shep gave her a quick wave good-bye, clearly anxious to get to work with his new friend, Abraham.

"Come on, Willa, it's just you and me," Jennie said to her daughter. "Let's help with the cleanup, then we'll collect Scout and head home."

The thirteen-year-old, Nan, overheard and came closer to them, directing her words to Willa. "If you would like to stay here, we can do something soon, after the chores."

Willa hesitated, then cast her eyes downward. "That's okay. I kind of have homework to do."

Jennie's heart sank. Her daughter didn't have homework that couldn't wait until later or tomorrow. She just wasn't comfortable enough to stay.

"Another time, right, honey?" Jennie put in.

"Yeah, sure."

"Okay." Nan smiled and left, not seeming to read too much into Willa's lukewarm response.

When they got outside, Jennie turned to Willa as she attached Scout's leash to his collar. "Didn't you want to stay?" she asked. "Maybe get to know Nan better? I mean, she's the same age and all."

Willa looked at her mother in annoyance. "Could you not get involved in everything I do, please? I won't make friends just because you tell me to. I'm not three years old, you know."

Oh, how I wish you still were, Jennie said to herself, thinking back to the happy baby her daughter had been. What a lovely idea.

In bed later that night, Jennie caught up on some sewing while waiting for Tim to get home. It had been such a pleasant day, she thought, replaying the meal at the Fishers'. When her son got back, she would get the whole story out of him about how he had met Peter. She wondered what they did after dinner. Maybe when the weather got warm, Peter would teach Tim to fish or something like that—give him a hobby or a new skill. It all made her feel more positive than she had in weeks. Things were definitely on an upswing, she decided, reaching for a pair of Shep's pants to repair a hole in the pocket.

At last, she heard the door open and Tim's steps in the front hallway. She waited for the sound of him coming upstairs.

"Where have you been?" It was her husband's voice, and he sounded angry. He must have been sitting in the living room, so he was right by the front door.

"Out. What difference does it make?" Their son's tone held its usual defiance.

"You know you have to call if you're staying out late."

Jennie could picture her husband leaning against the doorjamb, his arms folded, a frown on his face.

"It's not late. It's only ten-thirty!" Tim's voice was rising.

"And you are only fifteen!" Shep was louder. "You can't just come and go as you please. Why didn't you answer your phone?"

Jennie was surprised to learn that Shep had been calling Tim. First, because she didn't realize he was keeping such close tabs on their son; and also because her husband must have forgotten that Tim never answered a call from them. This had been a huge bone of contention back in Lawrence, but it hadn't come up since they moved here, at least not until today. No doubt because Tim hadn't had any place to go at night.

"I didn't have my phone. I'm pretty sure I left it in your car."

That was a flat-out lie. Jennie had seen it sticking out of his back pocket when he was leaving the Fishers'.

Shep's tone was clipped. "I don't believe that."

"Of course not! You never believe me!"

Jennie shook her head in amazement at her son's moral outrage when his father was right not to believe him.

"What do you care what I've been doing?" Tim went on. "I know what you've been doing! Sitting here, watching TV, and getting drunk on your stupid beer. So if I was doing anything other than that, I'm one up on you!"

Jennie's eyes opened wide in shock. She knew how much Tim hated it when his father drank any alcohol at all, but she had never heard him confront Shep so directly.

"How dare you talk to me like that!"

Jennie slid down in bed and put the pillow over her head. She couldn't bear to listen to another word. The action immediately transported her back to the nights when she was a young girl and her parents would argue. She remembered so many nights taking refuge from the sound of their shouting under her pillow.

"Mom? They're at it again."

It was Willa at the bedroom door. Jennie snatched the pillow away from her face.

"Yes, sweetheart?" Of course her daughter would have overheard it as well.

"I hate this."

"I know, honey." Jennie moved over in bed and held the covers up to indicate that Willa should climb in. "Come on, we'll chat a bit, you and I, until they calm down. They're just blowing off steam."

Willa rolled her eyes at her mother's attempt to smooth things over, but she got into bed and snuggled up. Jennie wrapped an arm around her, distracted from the fight downstairs by the rare opportunity to have a gentle moment with her daughter. "I love you, angel," she whispered.

"Love you, too, Mom." Willa's eyes were closed.

They lay there in silence as the argument downstairs continued, finally reaching a crescendo that ended abruptly when Tim took the steps up three at a time and went into his room, slamming the door behind him.

Chapter 6

"Honey, do you want to send any cards?"

Willa regarded her mother with annoyance. "Why?"

Jennie lowered her eyes to the task at hand, addressing Christmas cards. She had spread out the cards, envelopes, stamps, and her address book on the kitchen table, and was surprised when her daughter voluntarily slipped into the chair across from her, although her face was half-hidden behind her laptop's screen.

"What do you mean, *why*? Because you feel like it and it's nice, I guess. It's an important holiday. A happy one." Jennie slipped another card from the box of twelve and tried to come up with something to write to Willa's homeroom teacher, whom she barely knew. "How about someone you go to school with here? I'm going to send one to the Fishers. What about Nan? She likes you and wants to be friends. It would be a nice overture if she got a card directly from you."

Jennie was disappointed by the way Willa continued to ignore any overtures Nan made in her direction. In the weeks since they'd had dinner at the Fishers' farm, Shep had struck up an ongoing friendship with Abraham, and nothing pleased Jennie more than seeing the two of them discussing farming while working on repairs to one of the Fishers' buggies or the Davises' broken window sashes; it was wonderful that Shep had someone besides her to talk to, a real friend. Jennie's affection for Mattie grew with every encounter. Even Tim and Peter had an ongoing friendship; at that moment they were out ice-skating with some of Peter's friends. Only Willa refrained from warming up to the gracious and kind Fishers.

The suggestion horrified Willa. "That's the dumbest idea ever. Kids don't send each other cards, Mom. As if I'm not already considered the dorkiest kid in my grade!"

The phone rang, and uncharacteristically, Willa jumped up to answer it, clearly relieved by the opportunity to put an end to the conversation. Jennie listened to her daughter's side of the conversation, which consisted only of sounds indicating she understood what she was being told. When she hung up, she came back to her seat.

"Dad's got someone coming by tonight to buy a bike for their kid. So he'll be home at, like, nine-thirty."

"But we're supposed to decorate the tree tonight. You guys can't start that late. It's a school night."

Willa shrugged. "He said to start without him."

"Should we put it off until tomorrow?"

Willa was already busy typing on the computer's keyboard and didn't raise her eyes from the screen. "I don't care."

Jennie's shoulders sagged. That was exactly the problem: Nobody in the family cared about much of anything. At thirteen, her daughter should still be excited to trim the tree, or a little bit disappointed that her father wouldn't be involved and the event might even be put off. Jennie pictured the tree they had purchased two days ago, sitting in the living room, shorter than what they used to buy and a lot scrawnier, but the best they could afford. Her hope was that it would look better once the decorations went up. She was making strings of popcorn and cranberries to help fill in the bare spots. Of course, something would have to make up for the fact that there wouldn't be any gifts under it. She and Shep had agreed not to spend money on gifts for each other, and they had given the children their presents of new bicycles back in October. Tim and Willa had made no secret of their disappointment, although Jennie pointed out that these were not free bicycles but had to be paid for by their father, even if they cost him less than the full price. The children seemed to feel they were entitled to bicycles as a needed form of transportation. The whole discussion had left her with a sour taste, and she dreaded having to revisit the subject when the empty space beneath the tree reminded everyone.

At least by the time Shep's brother, Michael, and his family arrived on Christmas Day, presents normally would have been opened and cleaned up anyway, so they wouldn't have to be aware of the situation. Jennie felt a quick clenching in her stomach when she thought about the upcoming visit. She was extremely fond of her brother-in-law and his two children, but his wife was a different matter. Having come from a dirt-poor background, Lydia was the kind of person who wanted no part of anything that smacked of her lowly past. This small, dilapidated house would be unacceptable, repugnant even, in her eyes. Jennie had been quite surprised when they accepted the invitation to come for Christmas, even though they'd done so with the understanding that they would stay in a hotel and come only for Christmas dinner. After Michael and Lydia moved with their two children to Chicago four years ago so Michael could join a top law firm, she and Shep had seen little of them. Jennie was already checking out recipes and trying to come up with creative but inexpensive ways to make the house look festive. She would do her best to make the visit a warm, pleasant one, not like the awkward Thanksgiving of two years ago, the last time they had been together.

It hadn't always been this way. Unlike his wife, Michael was genuinely fond of Jennie. She had thought of him almost like her own younger brother and loved talking to him and having him around. For his part, Michael idolized his older brother and consulted him on every major decision he made in life— until it came to marrying Lydia. He must have sensed Shep wasn't a fan, so the first time they knew the wedding was taking place was when they received an invitation. After that, he no longer asked Shep about much of anything. Clearly, his wife was his new adviser. That didn't bother Jennie, because it made perfect sense that a husband and wife would decide things together. Still, the phone calls started to come less frequently, and efforts to see or even communicate with Shep and his family slowed to a trickle. She knew that Shep missed their old closeness and sensed his younger brother pulling further away over time. No doubt Lydia viewed them as the embarrassing hick relatives, though there wasn't anything Jennie could do about that. She tried to be warm and welcoming to all of them. If her sister-in-law didn't wish to reciprocate, then she would do her best to maintain whatever contact she could for the sake of her husband and children. It was just a bit difficult for Jennie to stomach the phony cheeriness of her sister-in-law, the condescension in her transparent efforts to make it seem like she cared for any of her husband's relatives. As fond as Jennie was of her niece and nephew, Lydia had zero interest in Tim and Willa and didn't pretend to. Perhaps that was what bothered Jennie the most.

She turned to the subject at hand. "We could do some of the tree tonight and some tomorrow night. How's that?"

Her daughter looked bored. "Whatever." Willa picked up the laptop, evidently deciding she had spent more than enough time with her mother. Jennie watched her exit, then tossed down her pen and shoved all the papers before her to one side. Folding her arms on the table, she put her head down and turned her face to stare out the kitchen window. She considered her lonely daughter, her disaffected son, and her beleaguered husband. She thought of the time and money she was about to put into what would, despite her hopes, undoubtedly turn out to be a grim Christmas Day. For several minutes she sat that way, unmoving.

"Oh, boy," she finally whispered. "Ho, ho, ho."

Christmas Day was frigid, with only a light dusting of snow on the ground. When she heard car doors opening, Jennie stopped into the small downstairs bathroom to run a brush through her hair and inspect her reflection, smoothing down the front of her long black skirt and red knit top. As she hurried to greet Michael and his family, Scout trotting behind her, she took a final look around, satisfied that the house was as clean as it could possibly be. The Christmas decorations had been up for the past few weeks, so she had dusted them as well. Everything from the wreath on the front door, the collection of Santas that she and Shep had started when they first married, and the decorations the children had made over the years were all neatly displayed.

Opening the front door, she saw Michael and Lydia standing beside a gleaming black car. Her brother-in-law wore a long overcoat and reflective sunglasses. Lydia was wrapped in a magnificent deep brown fur coat, her blond hair an artful mess. In her high-heeled leather boots, she was at least five feet eight, and it appeared she had lost weight since the last time they had been together. That would make her what, Jennie thought, about forty pounds total?

Lydia gathered up the children as Michael retrieved several packages from the trunk. When Jennie called out a greeting,

Michael turned to her with a big grin. They were coming inside as Shep hurried downstairs from the bedroom, freshly showered and rolling up the sleeves on his button-down shirt. He and Michael hugged and thumped each other on the back, while Jennie observed her sister-in-law looking around. Lydia's displeasure was indicated in an ever so slightly raised eyebrow, followed by an almost-imperceptible face indicating that she smelled an unpleasant odor.

"Welcome to our mansion," Jennie said with no trace of irony. "Come in and relax."

Beaming as if she could imagine nothing more delightful, Lydia took a step forward but was pushed aside by her son and daughter. "Aunt Jennie!"

They were both shouting her name as they hurled themselves against her. Scout barked in excitement, adding to the general chaos. Jennie knelt to embrace both children at once, remembering when her own were small enough to be hugged at the same time. Evan and Kimberly were seven and six, and Jennie had spent a great deal of time with them when they lived closer. She still sent them birthday cards but had no other contact and was looking forward to getting reacquainted.

"How about some hugs for your old uncle?" Shep extended his arms, and the children ran to him next. There was a lot of tickling and shrieking before everyone settled down.

"May I take your coat?" Jennie extended an arm toward Lydia and was rewarded with the impossibly soft fur coat draped across it. Lydia wore a beige cashmere dress with a narrow belt and small diamond earrings, as glamorous as if she had just left a magazine photo shoot. Everything she had on looked frighteningly expensive.

Michael came over to hug Jennie and kiss her cheek. "How's my favorite sister-in-law?"

"I'm great." Jennie took his coat from him, observing his neatly pressed khaki pants and navy blazer. "You look terrific, Michael." Her praise was genuine. "We're so glad you could come."

"I had to see your new life. So what do you think?"

"We have lots of time to talk about it," Shep said. "Let's get comfortable."

He threw an arm around Michael's shoulders and led him to the living room, their heads together as they fell into conversation. Jennie was relieved to see no awkwardness between them. She turned to find Lydia just about done helping her children out of their parkas and boots.

"Kids, go get Tim and Willa down here," Jennie told them. She hoped her children would make some effort to be nice to their little cousins, who ran upstairs, chattering noisily.

Lydia retrieved the contents of a large shopping bag and approached with two large gifts wrapped in glossy red paper and enormous gold bows. "Makeup for Willa," she said conspiratorially. "Tons of stuff in one giant kit, super-cool colors of eye shadow, blush, everything. For Tim, I got a cable-knit pullover. Bright royal blue—gorgeous."

Jennie tried to keep her expression neutral. Willa hadn't yet expressed the slightest interest in wearing makeup, nor would she have been allowed to even if she had. Tim wouldn't be caught dead in a sweater like the one Lydia was describing. Somehow, though it was rude, Jennie would have to make the gifts disappear until their company had left; her children were terrible at hiding their feelings when opening a present, and their faces would instantly reveal their distaste. To be fair, Lydia and Michael didn't have older children, so they couldn't know how to shop for them. On the other hand, she couldn't help thinking, if their aunt had ever bothered to find out the first thing about either one of them, she might have had an idea of what would be appropriate. What made Jennie feel worse was that she had spent more than she reasonably could afford on presents for Evan and Kimberly, yet these two gifts had probably cost five times as much.

The tournament of humiliation was just beginning.

Stop it, she silently commanded. Lydia had taken the time and trouble to select generous gifts. "That was very kind of you."

The other woman waved a manicured hand. "Nonsense. Now let's go look at your tree."

She took Jennie's arm as if they were close buddies, and they went into the living room. In the end, Jennie had done most of the tree decorating herself over a few days. She was rather proud of the total effect, with an angel Willa had made in fourth grade perched precariously but triumphantly on top. Looking at it through Lydia's eyes, she could see it was spectacularly unimpressive.

"Fabulous," Lydia said. "I love the adorable homemade touches. *Different* from what you usually see, you know?"

Ignoring the smoothly worded slight, Jennie pointed to the

trays of cheese and crackers and dip with cut-up vegetables set out on the coffee table. "Please have something," she urged.

"Looks delicious." Lydia smiled but seated herself as far away from the food as she could, perching on the edge of the chair.

That's why she can fit into that dress, Jennie thought, grabbing a cracker and cutting a thick slice of Jarlsberg cheese to go on it. "Drink?" she asked as she popped the cracker into her mouth.

"Sparkling water would be great."

"I'm sorry, but we don't have that. I can offer you water, soda, or wine."

"Water is fine. With a twist of lemon, please."

We are not *twist of lemon* people, Jennie wanted to say, but she left and went toward the kitchen. Maybe she would get lucky and find a lemon hidden in the back of the vegetable crisper. Or maybe she would get lucky and *turn into* a lemon who could hide in the back of the vegetable crisper. That would be even better.

An unbidden image came to her of Mattie Fisher, standing in her kitchen in black-stockinged feet, stirring an enormous pot of something steaming hot that smelled delicious. She was probably feeding a hundred people today, or some such impossible number. Without a doubt, she was placid yet in control, her movements efficient and certain. Jennie felt calmer just picturing it.

Thinking about the Fishers' accepting natures, it dawned on her that her own nature left something to be desired. She was the one ready to pounce on Lydia's every word. Whatever her sister-in-law was thinking, she was doing her best to keep it to herself. It was Jennie who was looking for insult at every turn. Maybe Lydia didn't love being there and was struggling to hide her disdain, but she was trying to be pleasant about it. Jennie could choose not to look for the jibe she feared behind every sentence. Instead of viewing Christmas as a time for the family to be happily together, she had made it all about her own insecurities over their situation. Who was at fault here?

Chastened, she mentally sent Mattie a "Merry Christmas" wish and a thank-you for unknowingly straightening her out. She pulled open the refrigerator door, resolving that when she went back into the living room, she was going to start over again and do it right.

Just then Shep appeared in the kitchen and reached across her to grab four cans of beer from the refrigerator door. Her heart sank. "You need all four right now?" The words were out before she could stop herself.

"It's easier to take them in now so I don't have to come back." Annoyance was evident in his tone. "Lighten up, Jennie. It's Christmas."

Apparently, Christmas meant different things to everybody in this family. None of them good. And none of them the right things.

The rest of the day passed in an exhausting blur. Conversations would start out well, then trail off into awkward silence as the differences between the two families became obvious in everything from incomes to values. Jennie was supremely disappointed in the kind of person Michael had become. He merely sat by while Lydia bragged about ski trips to Aspen, renovating their enormous apartment in downtown Chicago, how good their children's private schools were, and how well they would be positioned later for entry into a top college. Where, Jennie wondered, was the Michael she once knew? The down-to-earth, joking Michael who had taken such a loving interest in Tim and Willa? She could see her thoughts reflected in Shep's eyes, and despaired to observe the pace of his beer consumption pick up, not from any celebratory motive but from his obvious desire to block out what he was witnessing.

Even Kimberly and Evan were unrecognizable as the sweet small children she remembered; they were boisterous, demanding, and had no interest in anything other than what they wanted at a given moment. Evan spent much of the meal playing games on his cell phone, while Kimberly pushed her food around on her plate, complaining that the turkey wasn't the way she liked it and the vegetables were "icky." Jennie knew her own children were far from perfect, but at least they had been polite guests when they were little. Even as cell phone–obsessed teenagers, they knew better than to bring a phone to the table. She shuddered to imagine what kind of teens Kimberly and Evan would become.

If there had been any chance Shep might have opened up to his brother about their difficulties in adjusting to their new life, it was gone by the time they got to dessert. He refused the cake, ice cream, and cookie assortment, preferring to sit with yet another newly opened can of beer. When the younger children had finished their sweets, they told their mother they wanted to go back to the hotel to play video games.

"They're tired," Lydia said with an apologetic look to Shep and Jennie. "We'd better get back."

How sad, Jennie thought, that no one bothered to protest. Coats and boots were retrieved, kisses were exchanged among the four adults, and the other Davis family headed out the door. Michael was the last to leave, deliberately, Jennie realized, because he stuffed a heavy cream-colored envelope in her hand as he leaned in for an extra good-bye kiss on her cheek.

"What's this?" Jennie asked.

"Christmas card," he said. "We never got around to sending them out. But this one is for your eyes only."

He winked at her and left, pulling the door shut behind him. Jennie turned to see Shep retreating into the living room, knowing he would spend the rest of the evening sitting on the couch watching television, beer can in hand. Willa and Tim had disappeared upstairs. She would have to argue with them to get some help cleaning up. Before she did that, though, she wanted to see why Michael would have given her a separate holiday card.

She pried open the envelope with her thumb as she walked toward the dining room table to start clearing dishes. Instead of a card, she found a piece of stationery folded over. As she opened it, she caught her breath. Inside were hundred-dollar bills. She counted them. Twenty all together. Two thousand dollars. She read what Michael had written on the monogrammed paper.

Dear Jennie,

We both know my brother is stupidly stubborn and won't accept anything from anybody. So won't you do me the kindness of accepting this as our present to you? It's a combination housewarming (a little late, I know) and Christmas gift, and I hope it makes up for other gifts we've missed giving over the years. Of course, Shep is incalculably rich—he's got you and the wonderful family the two of you have created.

Love you always,
Michael

Stunned, she sank down onto one of the dining room chairs. This was the Michael she knew, the kind and loving one she now realized she missed terribly. Maybe he couldn't help showing off his newfound wealth, but underneath he knew his brother was hurting. Tears stung her eyes. She was ashamed that they needed this help, and ashamed that she didn't dare return the money because they were in such dire financial straits. Yet she couldn't help feeling a flood of relief that they had received another respite from disaster. Overshadowing everything else was the saddest thought: that she already knew she was going to follow Michael's unspoken advice and keep it a secret from Shep. More secrets, more walls between them. She folded the money back into the note and slipped it into the envelope, which she set down on the food-stained tablecloth. Then she covered her face with both hands and cried.

Chapter 7

Jennie put the paint roller in its tray and straightened up, rubbing her lower back. She had been painting Willa's bedroom for the past two hours. Thanks to Shep's prepping over the weekend, she was able to apply the off-white paint to smooth walls, and they were already looking fresh and clean after just one coat. Some bright white for the window frame and ceiling, and the room would be transformed. She smiled with satisfaction. Thanks to her brother-in-law's generous gift, after this she would paint Tim's room and then buy some desperately needed new linoleum for the kitchen.

Willa's room had come first, as Jennie figured her daughter could use a little lift by having it made more cheerful. She was looking more lost with every passing week. There was no sign of her making friends, nor had she come up with any activity at school that she wanted to join. So far, her grades had been acceptable, but just barely. Jennie was growing seriously concerned about her child's utter lack of interest in anything other than the computer. She had gone as far as taking away the laptop on several weekends, but that resulted only in her daughter becoming outraged and refusing to speak to her. Even if they could have afforded to give her lessons in something that appealed to her, it would have been a difficult task to figure out what that something might be.

Jennie sneezed. She had opened the window to dispel paint fumes, and frigid winter air filled the room. A snowstorm three nights ago had left the area blanketed in white; by now the snow was dirty and hard. When she and Scout went out that morning, he kept slipping on the icy road, so she curtailed their usual walk, promising to take him out more frequently for shorter durations. Looking at her watch, she realized she owed him an outing right about now.

As she shut the front door behind her, Scout tugging at the leash, she had a sudden desire to stop in at Mattie's. The Fishers didn't have a phone, so it wasn't possible to call before visiting, but they had made it clear the Davises were welcome to come by any time. As she now knew, if Mattie or Abraham were working on something—and when weren't they? she thought—they would continue, but their guest was welcome to stay or, even better, pitch in. Being able to help Mattie hang wet laundry on the line made Jennie feel a lot more comfortable about appearing unannounced, and she was thrilled that she and Shep were treated with such familiarity. Besides, she was delighted to do anything at all to lighten Mattie's load of housework, which was a thousand times greater than her own.

What invariably surprised her was how pleasant it was to do the work at their house, with its regular rhythms and order. While no one wasted time, the typical stress and the desire to finish that Jennie associated with housework were noticeably absent. Every job was as important as every other job, and the task wasn't just something to get through. It was, she thought, like a flowing river, with no beginning or end. Her own view, she realized, was to assess how long something would take and when she would be forced to do it again. The Amish seemed to understand that everything on the farm and in the household was connected and had its place in the weekly or monthly cycle. Instead of rushing, appreciate. What, she wondered, would it take to think that way?

Shep enjoyed his visits with Abraham so much that he was, she noticed, finding some extra free time for them. Occasionally, he went over early enough to help with the morning milking. It surprised her, because he was already so exhausted, he couldn't really afford to give up the extra sleep, and it wasn't helping him sell bicycles, but she could hardly begrudge him something he obviously found relaxing. What troubled her was that he preferred to escape to the Fisher farm rather than talk to her about how they could improve their financial situation. Not to mention the emotional distance between the two of them, expanding by the week.

"Am I going to have to storm the shop so he'll let me do some work there?" she asked Scout.

He was too busy sniffing and racing around the front yard to answer. After a while, they got into the car, and she drove to the Fisher farm. Just the walk from the car to the house left her shivering as Scout barked outside the now-familiar door.

"Come in." Mattie was ironing in a corner of the kitchen, as usual wearing black stockings but no shoes under her jewel-toned dress and black apron. Jennie had learned that, like other appliances here, the iron didn't run on electricity but on propane.

Mattie smiled. "Good afternoon to you both. Come join me, please." She set down the iron and extended a hand. "Let me take your coat."

"No, I'm fine, really." Jennie watched Scout settle down by her feet. "It's really cold today. Much worse than yesterday, don't you think?"

Mattie looked a bit surprised. "I thought it was better. Not so windy. Should I make you some hot tea? Or hot chocolate?"

"Well, you have to give me something to do while I'm here, so I don't feel like I'm interrupting your work. But tea is the best idea I've ever heard."

The other woman laughed. "I do not believe that, but you are very welcome to have some. With a doughnut, if you want one."

"Do I smell something wonderful cooking?" Jennie turned toward the stove to see a large pot on the burner.

"Bean soup. It will stay there all day. If anyone wants some, it is ready."

How homey, Jennie thought, immediately envisioning a welcoming pot of soup on her stove at home. Except that, in reality, no one would take any. She would have to eat it all. She smiled at the image of herself having to gulp down bowl after bowl of thick soup.

"What is funny?"

The two of them chatted comfortably for the next half hour, Mattie continuing to iron, Jennie carrying out an assignment of chopping onions. Some of the younger Fisher children came in and out of the kitchen, in the process of doing simple chores or to ask their mother a question. They greeted Jennie in their typical friendly fashion. Sarah, the fifteen-year-old, came to take the ironed laundry upstairs, then started preparations for the evening meal. In response to Jennie's inquiries, she explained that she was making ham and corn fritters. It turned out the chopped onions would be used for baked lima beans, to be combined with a mix of ingredients including molasses and brown sugar; it sounded delicious to Jennie, who asked if Sarah would give her the exact recipe another time.

"I'd be happy to. It's the least I can do to thank you for chopping the onions for me," Sarah told her.

"Anything I've eaten here has been so delicious. I'd love to know more about your cooking—your special dishes."

"If you want to see cooking, come back tonight and tomorrow," Sarah said with a smile. "We'll be preparing for a visit from our aunt and uncle. They're bringing their six children, and some of them come with their own children. So we'll have cakes and pies and lots of food."

"It is my sister and her husband," Mattie said. "They live forty miles from here."

"And they come in their horse and buggy?"

Mattie nodded. "Tonight they sleep at another sister's house that is in the middle. The winter is a time when we do a lot of visiting. Quieter on the farm."

"In the warm weather, there's not much time for that," Sarah added.

"Makes sense," Jennie said.

Suddenly, she noticed her body was aching all over, as if something had descended upon her and taken over, and despite the hot tea, she was actually getting colder. "You know," she said finally, "I'm not feeling quite right, and my skin has that crawly sensation. I'd better head home so you don't catch anything. Just in case."

Mattie looked concerned. "Let me give you some soup to take home."

Jennie realized she was getting a headache as well. "No, no, I'll be fine."

By the time she pulled into her own driveway and got Scout inside the house, she felt noticeably worse. She groaned inwardly at the thought of being stuck in bed for the next day or two. There was too much to do for that. Yet the effort it took to drag herself upstairs told her she might not have much choice in the matter. She managed to slip into a warm nightgown before getting into bed and yanking the quilt up to her chin, shaking with chills.

By the time her daughter got off the school bus, Jennie could barely raise her head from the pillow. Surprised to find her mother in bed, Willa came into the room to ask what was going on.

"Call Dad," Jennie said in a weak voice. "Tell him he needs to take charge of dinner and stuff."

Her daughter sounded alarmed. "Are you going to be okay?"

Jennie closed her burning eyes. "Of course," she whispered. "But now I need to sleep a little, okay, honey?"

When she opened her eyes again, she realized Shep was asleep in the bed beside her and it was dark outside. The house was silent. She had absolutely no idea what time it was. All she knew was that she felt like she was burning up. Groggily, she pushed off the quilt and reached toward the night table for her alarm clock, but the effort proved too much. She fell back against her pillow, miserable.

"Jen?" Shep stirred and spoke softly. "Are you all right? You've been dead asleep all evening."

"What time . . . ?"

He looked over at the clock on his side of the bed. "Three-twenty. In the morning. Do you want something?"

"So hot," was all she could manage.

"You must have a fever." He felt her forehead. "Whoa! Definitely." He got out of bed. "Let me get some aspirin."

It was all she could do to get the pills and water down her raw throat. He took the glass away and returned to put a cool washcloth across her forehead. She thanked him, not sure if she managed to speak the words aloud before falling back into a deep sleep.

She recalled only bits and pieces of the next few days, so sick that she was barely aware of her surroundings. The flu, Shep informed her, and a whopping case of it. She agreed. Every inch of her ached, her nose refused to stop running, and coughing fits left her in breathless pain. Her night table was an island of barely touched glasses of water, bowls of broth, tissues, and pills. It was the first time that she had been too ill even to inquire who was watching the children or taking care of the family's needs. At least, she thought in a more lucid moment, they weren't little anymore, so they could manage most things. Still, she couldn't muster the energy to say much to them when they came to her doorway, forbidden by their father to enter the sickroom. She endured the misery and waited for it to end.

It was nearly a full week before the worst was over, and she lay in bed for another two days, relieved to be better but too weak to do much. She was finally able to ask Shep what had been going on while she was essentially absent from their lives. It was a delightful surprise to find that Tim and Willa had pitched in to help their father. Shep had even finished the paint job in Willa's bedroom, and the two of them had rearranged her furniture. Both kids had made their beds every morning, fed themselves, and done the laundry.

"And your food?" Jennie asked. "Did you cook every night?"

Shep shook his head. "Never had to. The Fishers brought over dinner. Every day."

"What?" Jennie was shocked. "Mattie cooked for you guys?"

"Yup. I swear to you, I didn't ask for it, but she or one of her kids would come by in the buggy every afternoon and leave a meal. Tim had dinner at their place twice. We've been well fed, I promise you. Tonight we had fried chicken."

She couldn't get over it. With all Mattie had to do, she'd

made time to cook and deliver food to them daily, plus host Tim.

"Oh, she also asked if she could visit when you felt up to it."

Jennie smiled. "I'd love that. If I take it easy the rest of to-night, maybe tomorrow would work. And Shep . . ."

"Yes?"

"Thank you for taking such good care of me, and of every-body else. I'm sure it wasn't easy for you to manage it all."

There was a flash of his old smile, the dimple showing, and he bowed. "That's what I'm here for. Glad to be of service."

The next afternoon, she could hear the soothing clip-clop of a horse approaching, the sound growing louder until it stopped outside her window. A few minutes later, Mattie appeared, a heavy black shawl wrapped around her for protection from the cold. It startled Jennie to see her friend removed from her kitchen and transplanted to the Davis bedroom. The sight of Mattie in her bonnet standing beside a television, electric lights, and a telephone made no sense. Yet rather than Mattie looking out of place, it was the modern conveniences that seemed wrong.

"You are better?" she asked, coming forward and taking Jen-nie's hand.

"Much." Jennie gestured toward a chair.

Mattie nodded as she brought the chair closer to the bed and sat down. "Good. Your husband can stop worrying. Your children, too."

"They were really worried?"

"Oh, yes. They did not say, but it was in their eyes."

Between her family's helpfulness and concern, Jennie was touched. Even better, it justified her secret hope that the loving children she remembered were locked inside her cranky teenagers.

"Mattie, I don't know how to thank you. Shep told me about all the food you brought here."

She held up a hand. "Please. Your family needed you, and you needed some help. Very simple."

Simple for kind people like you, Jennie thought. Examples of such modest selflessness were few and far between. She wished with all her heart that she could be more like this woman. What was the secret?

"You even had Tim to your house to eat. He and Peter are becoming good friends?"

"I believe so."

"I'm so happy about that." Jennie hesitated. "Is this okay? I mean, because Tim's not Amish?"

Mattie turned to gaze out the window for a moment before turning her attention back and answering. "We are allowed to have friends who are not Amish, of course. We don't have too many, it is true. But Peter is in a different situation right now."

Jennie was confused. "In what way?"

"We believe that each person must choose to become Amish, and that is when he is baptized. As an adult, not as a baby. It is a decision each person must make. After that, a man or a woman follows all our rules and ways."

"I see."

"Have your ever heard the word *rumspringa*?"

Jennie shook her head.

"It is a word some people know, that is why I ask. When our children are teenagers, a little older, maybe sixteen, some want to go out into the English world a little more. This is what is called *rumspringa*." She gave Jennie a small smile. "Maybe they do some things we do not believe in."

"Can you tell me what, or is that a rude question?"

"They might listen to music and dance. Dress in English clothes sometimes. Not in their house or in front of their parents, no. Some use a cell phone or computer. Maybe even try alcohol."

"*What?*"

"Yes, that makes me very sad. I don't like to hear about the children doing this. We are not happy about it, but we understand. Remember, they have not been baptized into the faith yet, so they are not breaking their vows."

Jennie took this in. "Did you do any of these things?"

"I didn't need to. I wanted to marry Abraham, and I knew I wished to be Amish. Abraham was the same way, but he did drive a car for almost a year."

"A car? You're joking!"

"No. He didn't tell his parents, and he kept the car at an English friend's house. We are allowed to ride in cars, you know, though we cannot drive or own them. He did."

They sat while Jennie mulled over this information.

"It sounds very smart to me," she said. "This way, when they decide, they're ready. They've had a chance to experience what they're missing, so they won't continue wanting to try it."

Mattie looked grim. "Yes, but we worry if the children will make the right decision. If they don't decide to get baptized, then they are not Amish."

"Hmmm." Recognition dawned in Jennie's eyes. "Peter is sixteen."

A nod. "And he has five sisters born after him. His brothers are only five and four years old. Too young to help him and my husband on the farm. Peter must manage a lot of work. Responsibility. That is how it should be, but sometimes I think he is not so happy about this. It will get better for him."

"I'm sure. At his age, it probably seems like too much."

"Truly, Peter needs a wife to help him if he is to run the farm. He needs to join the church and marry." Mattie suddenly sat straighter in the chair, looking flustered. "Listen to me, telling you these things! What am I thinking of? Let us not talk of such nonsense."

"But . . ." Jennie was confused by her friend's retreat.

"I left some turkey soup downstairs for you. Shep tells me you have not been eating very much. I hope the next time I see you, your cheeks will be rosy again." Mattie got up to go. "If you or the children need anything, you will tell me."

"You've already done too much."

"No. You must get all better. Please."

With a quick wave, she was gone. Jennie stared at the doorway, wondering what had transpired. She was happy that Mattie had confided in her, but apparently, the other woman had gone further than she'd meant to in talking about her son. Jennie also wondered if Tim was involved in any of Peter's so-called English activities. Obviously, the boys were spending time together, but she hoped they weren't doing anything that might cause Mattie or Abraham distress. It seemed they were usually at the Fisher farm, and she couldn't imagine they could get into much trouble there. Maybe he was lending Peter his cell phone or computer. At fifteen, Tim was too young to drive, so he couldn't lend Peter a car or drive him someplace he shouldn't go. She made a mental note to talk to her son about all this as soon as possible.

It had been a special treat to have Mattie come to her house, but Jennie was so weak that the visit had worn her out. She closed her eyes and slept.

Chapter 8

It was quiet in the house, with Willa in her room and Tim over at the Fishers'. Jennie sat at the kitchen table, turning the pages of the supermarket's weekly circular with one hand and jotting notes on a pad with the other. On Sunday nights she planned her food shopping for the week, coordinating specials and coupons. It would have been nice, she thought, if Shep ever sat there with her, doing his weekly review of his business expenditures. They could have had companionship, even if they didn't speak. Yet he preferred to do his work alone in the living room. He might as well be in another country, she mused.

The phone rang, and Jennie got up. Willa rarely bothered to answer a landline, assuming that if anyone wanted to speak to her, they would call her cell phone.

"Hello?"

Tim's voice was frantic. "Mom, you gotta come! It's Abraham."

She was instantly alert. "Abraham? What's the matter?"

"He's—Mom—he's dead!"

She caught her breath. "No, Tim, no, he can't—"

"He is, I swear. He collapsed. Right here in the kitchen. It was awful! I saw it!"

For a moment she couldn't speak. "Is Mattie there now?"

"Everybody's here. Can you come?"

"On my way."

She hung up and rushed into the living room. "Shep, I don't believe it."

He was sitting on the sofa and looked up from the papers in his lap.

"Abraham died. Tim just called. I'm going over there."

"What? He *died?*" He got up, shock on his face. "I'm coming, too. What happened?"

"I don't know." She grabbed her jacket from the hall coat closet and called out to her daughter, deciding it would be best to say nothing just yet about what had happened. "Willa, we're going to the Fishers' for a bit. Will you be okay?"

"Sure," came the muffled reply.

Jennie and Shep raced to his truck and sped off to the farm. She repeated what Tim had said on the phone, but it didn't explain much. They pulled up to the farm to see two horses and buggies tied up in front of the barn. When Shep yanked open the kitchen door, they were met by the sight of Mattie sitting in a chair, the room quiet and dim. Becky, Aaron, and Moses, the three youngest Fisher children, sat at her feet, their heads buried in her lap. Several Amish women moved about in the kitchen, making coffee or tea, and preparing food. No one said a word. The room was illuminated by only a few lanterns, and the darkness added weight to the silent sorrow.

Jennie froze. Perhaps she didn't belong here at such a time. Maybe only other Amish were wanted or would know what to do. Mattie turned reddened eyes toward her and nodded.

"Oh, Mattie," Jennie whispered, coming forward. "Then it's true? Abraham—"

"Yes." Her voice was barely audible.

Peter came into the room, his face ashen, one arm around his eight-year-old brother, Joshua, who appeared more bewildered than anything else, the other around ten-year-old Emma, her face tearstained. Tim was right behind them, and his eyes flashed gratitude at the sight of his parents.

"What can I do?" Jennie whispered to her son. "What do they need?"

He shrugged. "There's a doctor on the way. It's too late, but they have to get one here, I guess. They think it was a heart attack."

"Where is . . . Abraham?" Shep asked his son.

"One of the bedrooms, I think."

Jennie winced and went over to Mattie. "Please tell me what to do for you."

The other woman's expression was stoic but exhausted. "Do not worry about me. There are many people to care for us now. In three days, you will come when we have the burial, please. Yes?"

"Of course. I'm here if you need anything."

Jennie reached out to lay her hand over Mattie's for a moment, then turned and motioned to Shep and Tim. The three of them left the house together.

"I can't believe this, I can't," Jennie burst out when they got to the truck.

"He just kinda crumpled up, but you could tell he was in pain," Tim said. "It looked like slow motion, you know?"

"Poor Abraham." Shep's lips were set in a grim line.

"Were the children around?"

"Just Peter and me. We were talking to him. Well, Peter was. About wheatgrass or something."

"What happens now?" Shep wanted to know.

"Peter said he goes to the funeral place, and I guess they fix him up. Then they keep him at home, and they'll have a funeral in a few days."

"I'm so sorry you had to see that," Jennie told her son. "It must have been upsetting."

"Well, *duhh*."

Jennie began to turn around in her seat, angered by his rudeness, but Shep caught her eye and made a conciliatory face to tell her to let it pass. He was right, she realized. Tim was no doubt frightened, and it was logical that he would lash out.

The next day Jennie saw numerous buggies parked outside the Fisher house whenever she drove or walked by. She dropped off a stew and a dozen muffins, but as she'd expected, the kitchen was virtually overflowing with food provided by the Amish neighbors. As Mattie had selflessly provided for Jennie when she had needed support, her neighbors were doing the same for Mattie.

It made Jennie sad to contemplate how few people would be there for her own family in the event of a crisis. Human connection, she thought, was the most important thing, and it was missing even within her household. Especially within it. They weren't there for one another. That night, when she and the children sat down to eat, she served a few of their favorite foods and tried to foster some conversation. It didn't take more than five minutes for them to start fighting, and the meal ended with Tim grabbing his food and silverware and stomping off to his room to get away from his sister. She quickly finished, then got up wordlessly and left the room. Another wonderful evening, Jennie thought as she scraped the leftovers into the garbage.

Two days later, Shep closed the bike shop, and he and Jennie went to the funeral. In front of the Fisher house, buggies lined the street in both directions. The simple wooden coffin was in the living room, and Mattie and the children sat next to it. Hundreds of people had come, and they filed through to see Abraham, dressed in white, his head and chest revealed by two open hinged pieces on the coffin. Mattie sat with great dignity as friends and family came past. Jennie was amazed at the quiet among such an enormous group, murmuring softly if they spoke at all. When it was time for the service, she followed the women, who seated themselves on benches separate from the men. There was no eulogy, no testimonies about Abraham's life; it was more of a church service than what she'd expected.

An enclosed carriage brought the coffin to the cemetery, followed by a stately procession of horses and buggies. As they walked from their car, Jennie and Shep noted the plain tombstones in the cemetery, marked only with a name, the dates of birth and death, and the person's age in years, months, and days. They couldn't see Mattie or the children, who stood at the center of a sea of Amish relatives and visitors. At one point, Jennie caught a glimpse of Peter, pale and with an expression she could only interpret as panicked.

There was no singing, just a hymn read as the coffin was lowered into the ground and covered with dirt. Jennie cried softly for the loss of this kind man and the hardship it would cause Mattie and her children. When the burial was complete, everyone was directed to say the Lord's Prayer in silence. Then it was over. Some of the guests returned home, while others went to the Fishers'.

"Simple and spare, like Abraham himself," Shep murmured as they got back into their car.

"Peaceful," Jennie replied. "It was beautiful, although they probably wouldn't like that description. But to me, it was."

"The way these people live is so . . ." Shep trailed off.

"I know."

He smiled at the way she understood without his having to explain, then turned the key in the ignition. Oh, my sweet husband, she thought as she watched him, in so much emotional pain and so far away from me. She reached out to touch his face. He looked at her in surprise, then gently took her hand and turned it over to kiss the palm.

Over the next weeks, it was obvious to Jennie that Shep was mourning the loss of his friend. He was more withdrawn than usual, and sadness was evident in his eyes. In the early mornings, he went over to help with the morning milking. On weekends, he went back, assisting the other Amish men who were there to keep the farm operating as usual. When she tried to discuss how Shep felt about losing Abraham, though, she got little response. Jennie tried to visit Mattie often, but invariably found the house crowded with family members or friends. Mattie was always glad to see Jennie, although they didn't have any time alone. Jennie tried to gauge how her friend was holding up. She appeared tired and a bit thinner, but nothing in her expression gave away what she was going through. With the children, she remained decisive and in charge. Jennie envisioned eight baby birds, all needing food and care from their mother. And she was always right there for them.

On one visit, Mattie did find a moment to explain to Jennie that Abraham's brother and his family would be staying with them, at least through the fall. Efraim Fisher had his own carpentry business, but he and his wife would come to help Peter with the farm until they all decided on a long-term plan. Everyone understood that Peter would take over the farm, but he couldn't manage it alone, and they would have to plan for the future.

"That's wonderful," Jennie said when she heard the news. "And Abraham's brother is able to leave his own business?"

Mattie nodded. "His eldest son and daughter-in-law will manage. Efraim has another grown son who will come also and will bring his wife and children. They are actually about to move, so they have agreed to stop here for a while before they go on. It will be very good for all of us. Many more hands. And best, I think, for Peter. The spring and summer are so busy on the farm."

Jennie considered the disruption this other family would be undergoing. She could only marvel at the loyalty and selflessness of people willing to be uprooted that way.

Then, startling her, the image of her sister, Hope, flashed across her mind. It had been years since she had allowed herself to think of the sister who had chosen never to see her again. Yes, she had sent money that had been a lifeline for Jennie back when she lived at home with their mother. What she remembered most clearly, though, was Hope's cruelty in disappearing without a word, making sure she couldn't be found. Jennie had pushed that hurt as far away as she could, but she had never been able to get rid of it.

It dawned on her that somehow, without realizing it, she had come to view a family as people tied together by blood rather than love. After her father had left, her mother, her sister, and she had been such a family. She thought of the bonds between her husband and his brother, Michael, once so strong, getting weaker every year. Now she and Shep and the children were starting to feel like the same kind of unit: bound by obligation, no one willing to open up or ask anyone else to help with their dreams or even their needs.

The Amish might not spend a lot of time talking about what they needed, but they didn't have to; they *acted*—to assist, to protect, to support one another. She had seen it every time she came by. It was in the way they all carried out an unending list of chores without complaint, or how the children took care of one another, whether an older sister helped a younger one put on her shoes, or several of them sat, examining flowers and bugs outside in the sunshine, talking about what they were seeing. It was also in the way they gathered every other Sunday to worship in someone's home, committed to their faith, their community, their families. She knew from the Fishers' modesty that they did not brag about what they did or draw attention to themselves in any way. They just did what needed doing and seemed all the stronger for it.

From their doing came strength. Jennie knew there was a lesson in there for her, but she wasn't sure what it was.

Chapter 9

The raspberry preserves from a local farm had become a favorite of Shep's. Jennie decided to buy two jars, since she didn't get to the marketplace that often. An elderly Amish woman took her money with a solemn expression, but Jennie wished her a good day and was gratified to receive a small smile in return. She settled the jars into her net shopping bag, thinking she might as well pick up some dried green peas while she was here.

When she got to the end of the aisle and turned the corner, she stopped in surprise. There was a booth she had seen many times before. She had bought a few of their freshly baked pies and breads in the past. What surprised her was that the person behind the counter today was Mattie.

Waiting until her friend finished taking care of a customer, Jennie approached. Mattie's face brightened when she saw who it was.

"Wow, this is a new development," Jennie said. "I had no idea you were working here."

"I started last week. It is really the booth of my aunt and uncle. They went to Ohio for a few months to visit my aunt's family, so I am running the booth for them."

"Do you bake all this?" Jennie gestured to the array of pies, breads, coffee cakes, and her own favorite, sticky buns.

"Oh, no. The family does the baking. I pick it up in the morning and bring it. Then I work here to sell it."

A woman behind Jennie tapped her shoulder in annoyance. "Are you going to talk much longer? I'd like to buy something."

Taken aback by the woman's rudeness, Jennie wondered if she might actually be taking up too much time. Perhaps the slower pace of life here had slowed her down as well. That didn't seem like such a bad thing, she thought. Not wanting to ruin Mattie's chance to make a sale, she apologized and backed away with a wave.

"We can visit later," Mattie called to her before turning to the customer with her usual sweet smile.

Jennie resolved to take Scout on a walk to the farm that afternoon. She hadn't had a good visit with the Fishers in far too long. Ever since Abraham had died three months ago, the house had been busy with Amish friends, family members, and visiting relatives who had traveled from all over to get there. Plus, there were the members of Abraham's family who had moved in, which turned an already busy house into what felt to Jennie like a small hotel. Fortunately, there was plenty of room for everyone, due to the two additions that had been built over the years to house different generations. It was common among the Amish to live that way, Mattie had explained, grandparents and even great-grandparents residing with younger generations, yet having independence and privacy with their own kitchens and living facilities. Abraham's parents had both lived on the farm until their deaths a few years back, but their rooms had remained empty since then.

Well, the space was being put to good use, Jennie reflected. Having met the people who had come to stay with Mattie, she had been struck by how quickly they'd settled into a routine. Abraham's brother Efraim and his wife, Barbara, seemed to know at once what needed doing. They took care of things with little discussion and few questions. Jennie found them reserved with her but always kind. They had brought their grown son, Red, and his wife, Ellen, whose young children were as sunny-natured as Mattie's. She supposed Barbara and Ellen were watching all the children so Mattie could take this job. She could imagine them effortlessly handling such a big brood. It was barely spring, but Jennie had already seen these women working hard in the garden, and the men were out in the fields all day. Everyone there was incredibly busy.

Unlike her.

She walked to her car, thinking about how useless she was beginning to feel. Nothing further could be accomplished in her house without spending more money, which wasn't an option. The children were settled into their school routines, complaining at every turn and bickering with each other. Willa was still hiding out in her room, Tim was still fighting with his father. Shep continued to work long hours, although his business was picking up slightly as the warmer weather moved in, at least enough for them to get by if they watched every penny. Yet he kept his thoughts to himself and drank enough beer to get him through the nights, enough to make him numb to his own unhappiness. She knew that if he was on his way to becoming an alcoholic, he would drink more over time, not less. No one, she had to admit, was any happier than they had been before. They were merely treading water. Her contribution to fixing this mess was—what? she asked herself. Nothing. She seemed to have become paralyzed, uncertain what it was that her family needed to bring them together in some way.

Then there was Mattie. She had lost her husband and been left with a farm and eight children. Yet she didn't wallow in her sadness; she barely showed the emotional pain Jennie knew she was in. Occasionally, she would look off, sometimes lose track of what they had been discussing. In those moments, Jennie knew she was thinking of Abraham. Still, she refused to give in to her grief. Every day she got up and forged ahead. I need that kind of steel spine, Jennie thought.

When she arrived home, she found Willa had returned from school and was standing in front of the open refrigerator, mulling over what to choose for a snack. Scout was dozing under the kitchen table.

"How are you, honey?" Jennie asked Willa, setting down her bag on the counter. "Can I fix you something?" She pulled out her purchases and held them up. "Some dried peas with jelly, perhaps?"

"Very funny, Mom, thanks," Willa answered, taking an apple from the vegetable bin. She bit into it. "Ew, mushy. I hate that."

"It's apple season in the fall. That's when we get the really crunchy ones."

"Do I have to finish it?"

Jennie shook her head. "Leave it for me. I'll use it with the others to make applesauce."

"Thanks."

"Homework?"

"Not much."

"Why don't you take Scout for some exercise in the front yard? Throw him a ball."

At the sound of his name, Scout got up from under the kitchen table and came over to Jennie.

"Okay." Willa didn't sound excited, but she told Scout to come with her, and the two left.

Jennie could hear her daughter entreating the dog to fetch the old tennis ball they kept outside for this purpose. Deciding to set the table early, she opened the silverware drawer and was gathering forks when she heard Willa scream the dog's name in the front yard.

There was a screeching of car brakes, a moment of quiet, then another screech.

"No!" Willa shouted. "Scout!"

Jennie ran to the front door. Willa was kneeling by the dog, who lay on his side in the middle of the street. She looked up at her mother in horror.

"He was hit by a car," she shouted as Jennie raced over to them. Her voice took on the edge of hysteria. "He ran into the street to get the ball. I didn't mean to throw it there, I swear. And the man just drove away, really fast."

"It's all right, Willa, it's not your fault."

Jennie dropped to her knees. Come on, Scout, please, she begged silently, please be okay. The dog's eyes were open and he was breathing shallowly. At least he was alive.

"Stay here with him," she ordered Willa, running back into the house.

With shaking fingers, she frantically looked through the county phone book for the number of an animal hospital. She spoke to a nurse, then grabbed her car keys and drove the car closer to where Scout lay. They gently moved him into the backseat, his head on Willa's lap. Jennie sped to the vet's office as her daughter tried to talk soothingly through her tears to the whimpering dog.

"Will he be okay, Mom? Will he?"

"I hope so, honey."

When they got to the hospital, the staff took over, putting Scout on a gurney and wheeling him in at once for X-rays. Jennie and Willa were left to sit in the waiting room, both of them teary-eyed and afraid of the news they might get. A receptionist called Jennie over and handed her a clipboard, asking her to fill out the attached forms. As she made her way through the questions, her heart sank. No, she checked off, they did not have pet insurance. Yes, she and her husband were financially responsible for the dog and agreed to pay the charges incurred.

She left the completed forms on the desk and sat down, wondering what it was going to cost and how on earth they were going to pay. There was absolutely no room in their budget for such an emergency.

After a seeming eternity, the doctor came out to speak to them. "Your dog has a broken leg and some broken ribs, but we think he's going to be okay. We just have to finish with some of the other tests."

"Oh, Mom." Willa was overjoyed, and they both let out sighs of relief.

"The ultrasound indicates there's no internal bleeding. We've done blood work to check his organ functions. We'll keep him here—if everything checks out, I'm guessing it'll be for two nights. Let's talk tomorrow to discuss the next step."

Jennie thanked him. On the ride home, Willa and she were acutely aware of Scout's absence in the car and how close he had come to being killed. The house that night was far too quiet, in her opinion, not that Scout was prone to making much noise. Everyone was reflective for the next two days; no one even seemed to have the desire to argue.

At last it was time to bring Scout home. Jennie stood near the receptionist in the waiting room, and the doctor came out to see her. The family would need to give Scout pain medicine and keep him from extensive activity, but he should be fine after his leg and ribs healed. They were to change the bandage every few days and, after he was better in a few weeks, bring him back for a final check. Jennie thanked him and he left, saying Scout would be brought out but she should see the receptionist first.

The receptionist presented her with the bill.

She almost gasped aloud. Three thousand dollars. She ran her eye over the itemized charges. Tests, medicines, lab work, even a bandage change. It was a long, expensive list.

"How will you be paying for that, Mrs. Davis?" the receptionist asked.

With my life's blood, she wanted to say. She had no idea what she was going to do. She had about seven hundred dollars left from the money Shep's brother had given her, and she had decided to hold on to it for an emergency or, with any luck, put it toward college for Tim.

This qualified as an emergency, but even if she used the entire amount, it would barely make a dent in the bill.

The receptionist smiled, waiting for an answer.

"Is there someone I could talk to?" Jennie managed to get out. "About, you know, a payment plan or something like that?"

The smile disappeared as the woman reached for the phone. "I'll see if someone in billing can speak with you now."

Jennie sank down on one of the waiting room chairs, wishing she could crawl under it and hide. She couldn't remember the last time she had felt so embarrassed. Now she would have to grovel to make some arrangement, and she couldn't even guess what that might be. There wasn't any extra money coming in that could go toward the debt. She doubted the billing people would appreciate her promise to pay it off over ten or fifteen years.

She turned to gaze out the window, humiliated and furious at the same time. This was it. This was the limit. Trying to go along with Shep, letting him have his way about running everything alone, was one thing. Her agreeing to sit around and not work, an able-bodied person capable of holding a full-time job, was another. They needed a second income. Now. Whatever his difficulties with the idea of his wife working, they were no longer part of the equation. She was going to find a way to make some money. She would pay off this bill and make it so that every financial surprise didn't leave them teetering on the edge of calamity. In her heart, though, she knew this decision would make things between her husband and herself worse than they already were. If that was even possible.

Chapter 10

"There's a good boy."

Scout lay on the floor while Jennie removed his dirty bandage and replaced it with a fresh one, trying to move his injured leg as little as possible. When she finished, she stroked his back and murmured reassuringly to him. He put his head down and sighed, a sound that always made her and the children laugh because it seemed so human. She didn't laugh at the moment; she felt sorry for him, medicated and groggy, limping, and doubtless in discomfort from his broken ribs.

She tossed out the old bandage and sat down at the kitchen table to review her list. For the past few days, while everyone else was out of the house, she had been compiling ideas about what she might do to earn money. Her prospects were not encouraging. She wasn't proficient enough with computers to be an assistant in an office. Home shows selling kitchen tools or clothing were out because they required finding people to host shows and invite customers; she knew barely a soul here. She didn't have money to invest in inventory or fancy equipment. Nothing in the want ads seemed appropriate for her. She had spent hour after hour calling retail stores to see if there were any openings, but she'd come up with only a few part-time shifts at odd hours.

"Help me out here, Scout," she muttered to the dog. "There's an answer somewhere, so why can't I find it?"

She glanced over at him, snoring gently. "You've been through enough this week, old buddy. I shouldn't bother you with this stuff. It's just . . ."

Shaking her head, she put the list in a drawer where no one was likely to stumble upon it; no point in discussing any plans before they were fully formulated. It was time to concentrate on dinner. Tonight she was keeping a long-overdue promise to Tim to make a carrot cake like the one he had been served at the Fishers'; Mattie had given her the recipe back in the fall. She sighed, recalling that it was well before Abraham died. She opened the refrigerator, reaching for the carton of eggs. First she would mix the meat loaf and get that into the oven.

She heard the front door open.

"Tim?"

"Yeah, what?"

"Hi, honey. Come in here and tell me about your day."

Her son appeared in the kitchen doorway, his backpack slung over one shoulder. He was eating a candy bar, half unwrapped.

"What do you want to know?" He didn't look eager to talk.

"Anything you want to tell me."

"Boring day. Same as always." He held up the half-finished chocolate. "This is the best thing that happened to me all day. How's that for an exciting life?"

She smiled as she set the eggs down on the counter. "Candy is one of the simple joys of life. Everybody loves a day with candy in it." She stopped, the smile disappearing, her hand still on the egg carton. That was true, wasn't it? Everybody loved candy.

She could make candy and sell it.

Not that she knew anything about making candy, but surely she could learn. She envisioned trays with rows of chocolates and pastel confections, decorated in delicate lace designs of every color.

"Hello? Are you still with us?"

Her son's voice snapped her back to the present.

"Oh, sure, sorry." Tomorrow she would research the idea further, see if she was on to something or out of her mind to consider it. "Lot of homework tonight?"

He didn't answer but crossed the kitchen to stoop down next to Scout and scratch behind his ears. "They couldn't get rid of you so easily, eh, pal? You're a lot tougher than you look."

I hope the same is true of me, thought Jennie, or we're all going to be in big trouble.

The next day, she spent the better part of the morning online, looking up recipes and candy-making techniques. Then she went to the library to take out books on the subject. Spreading them out on the kitchen table, she compared recipes, lists of necessary equipment, and the level of difficulty for various categories of candy. There was a lot more to working with chocolate than she had realized, like understanding the different types to get the result you were going for, and tempering it. She decided the easiest place to start was something more elementary, finally selecting peanut brittle as a jumping-off point. No exotic ingredients were needed, although she would have to buy a candy thermometer, clearly a basic tool of the trade. The recipe required throwing a few things into a pot until it reached a certain temperature, spreading the mixture onto a flat pan, and letting it cool. Simple.

She jumped into the car and returned in under an hour with everything she needed. It seemed so easy, she thought, stirring the water, corn syrup, and sugar in a pot. When that started to boil, she added lots of Spanish peanuts and stirred some more. All she had to do was wait until it became a nice brown color, then add some baking soda. It was hard to tell exactly what color that should be, though. At last it started turning brown, but she wasn't sure if it was brown enough. She continued to stir, and the smell of burning peanuts filled the air. Her heart sank. She had waited too long.

Everything went into the trash. She hadn't anticipated such a total failure, so she had to go back to the store for more peanuts. This time she got at least three times what she needed, and began again. She reread the recipe, triple-checked to make sure everything was ready in advance, and watched the mixture like a hawk. When she felt certain the moment was right, she poured in the small amount of baking soda. The hot mixture expanded and bubbled up faster than she had anticipated, spilling over the top of the pan. It took her so long to clean up the gooey mess, she had to stop for the day; Willa would be getting off the school bus, and Jennie didn't want anyone to know what she was trying to do. She hurried around the kitchen, cleaning and putting away the ingredients before taking out the trash with her failed experiments. If she couldn't do this one simple recipe, she thought, there wasn't much hope for the future. Her visions of delicate chocolates and irresistible sugar creations receded into the distance.

The next morning, as soon as everyone had left, she was back at the stove. This time everything went smoothly. With a broad grin, she broke the cooled and hardened brittle into pieces. At least they looked like peanut brittle was supposed to look. She bit into one. Delicious. She let out a whoop.

"I did it!" she announced to Scout, who was snoozing nearby. "It actually tastes like peanut brittle."

He opened one eye, then shut it again.

"Oh. You're right," she said. "That wasn't nice, since I can't give you any."

She placed the pieces on layers of waxed paper, then into one of the decorative tin containers she had purchased. The next step was to get some consumers' reactions—those consumers being her children. She waited until they had finished dinner and were reluctantly clearing the dishes. It was just the three of them; as usual, Shep was working late.

As casually as she could manage, she brought out the tin of brittle and opened it. "Kids, I made this today. Do me a favor and tell me how it is."

Tim was closer to her and grabbed a piece. "I didn't know you could do this, Mom," he said as he chewed.

"But how is it?" She held the box out to Willa.

"Give me a minute, will ya? Why are you all nervous?" He took another bite. "You know, it's actually great. You did a fine thing here."

Willa gingerly nibbled at hers. "Yum. I mean, *yum*."

"Really?" Jennie asked. "You swear?" she said to Tim.

"Yes, I *swear*. What's with you?" Her son rolled his eyes and left the room, grabbing a second piece as he went by.

"I have a math test tomorrow," Willa said, heading out, peanut brittle in hand. "But thanks, this is awesome."

Alone in the kitchen, Jennie was pleased if not satisfied by their reactions. She had made it too obvious that she wanted their praise. At least Willa would have noticed that and made sure to say something nice; Tim was happy to eat pretty much anything, so his reaction was a bit suspect anyway. She needed a more objective opinion.

She checked the kitchen clock. Seven o'clock, not too late. Shouting out to the children that she would be right back, she drove to the Fishers' house. The dim light of their battery-operated lanterns and propane-powered lamps was visible through numerous windows. Mattie and her relatives were in their respective parts of the house, all busy with some chore or another, she guessed. A barefoot Emma came to see who was knocking on the door.

"Hello." She greeted Jennie with a smile. "Are you here to visit with my mother? She's sewing a new dress for Becky. She's already as big as me, so we don't have enough dresses for both of us!"

"Does your mother make all your clothes?" Jennie's curiosity momentarily trumped her purpose for being there.

"Yes." The little girl thought about it. "Not the hats for my brothers. But everything else I can think of."

Just another little hobby, Jennie thought, making the entire wardrobe for such a huge family.

"Should I tell her to come?"

"No, Emma, don't bother her if she's busy. I made this peanut brittle for all of you. Would you give it to your mother and tell her I hope you enjoy it?"

Emma reached out for the tin.

"Thank you," Jennie said. "Could you ask her something for me? I've never made it before, so I'd like to know if it tastes good or not."

The little girl gave a solemn nod and turned around to follow Jennie's instructions. Smiling, Jennie got back into her car. She would learn the truth about her peanut brittle soon enough.

She didn't hear anything the next day. It wasn't as if Mattie would call on the telephone, so that left either a visit, she told herself wryly, or a message sent by carrier pigeon. Early in the evening, unable to wait any longer, Jennie drove back to the farm. It was still light, and as she approached the house, she saw Mattie standing near the vegetable garden, talking with Peter and Sarah. She came around to where she was visible and called out hello.

"Jennie," said Mattie with pleasure, "I received your gift last night, but you did not come in. Why?"

"You were busy."

She frowned. "Not too busy to say thank you for a gift."

"It was nothing. But if you got a chance to eat it, I would really like to know your opinion. Did you like it?"

"It was good."

Peter and Sarah nodded in agreement.

"Yes. It was. I ate so much, my stomach hurt," Sarah said.

"I ate more than you, and my stomach was fine," Peter said. He glanced toward the barn. "Excuse me. I have to take a look at Maisie."

"A cow who is not so well," Mattie explained to Jennie as he walked away.

"And I'll get back to my sewing," Sarah said. "I'm working on a pillow cover." She said good night.

Jennie turned to Mattie. "You said you tried the peanut brittle?"

She nodded.

"And you liked it?"

"Yes." Mattie smiled.

Three for three, Jennie thought. She had her answer. The Amish weren't prone to hyperbole or empty praise. They didn't brag about what they did; nor did they go on and on giving anyone else compliments. When they said good, that was exactly what they meant. It was probably the highest praise she could have hoped for.

"You are worried that something was wrong with it?"

Jennie was overwhelmed with the need to confide in someone. "Mattie, I have to find a way to make some money." She paused. "We're pretty much broke. Shep works hard, but the store doesn't bring in enough."

Mattie looked sympathetic but didn't say anything.

"I came up with the idea of selling candy. So I made that to see if I could do it. I know it's not unique or anything, but still. That's what I'm really asking: Is it good enough to sell?"

Mattie considered the question. "Yes, it is."

The confirmation flooded Jennie with relief. "Now I have to figure out where to sell it."

The other woman frowned. "You have no place to do this?"

Jennie shrugged. "Not really. A stand by the road? I don't know what my choices are yet."

Mattie looked out over the garden, thinking. "What if I sold it at our booth at the market?"

"You would do that?" Jennie was taken aback by such a generous offer. She turned it over in her mind. "That would be fantastic, but why would your uncle allow me to sell something that might take business away from his food?"

"I would talk to him. I am thinking we would buy it from you and sell it for a profit. You would be a vendor, and we would buy your product from you. Simple."

A smile spread across Jennie's face. "Of course. I'll provide it to you, and you'll do the selling."

"Let me talk to my uncle's family."

Jennie gave her a quick hug. "I don't know how to thank you."

"Do not. He might say no. I am hoping it would be good for everyone."

"In the meantime, I'll practice making a better brittle." Jennie laughed, her excitement growing. "Have to come up with a bag or a box for it, and a name. So much to do!"

Saying their good nights, the women went in different directions, Mattie toward the barn, Jennie toward her car. Even if Mattie's uncle said no, even if Jennie came up with another place and the candy didn't sell, at least she would know she had tried. She was no longer sitting by and waiting for someone or something to come along and rescue the family. She was taking action, and it felt wonderful. Just knowing that gave her the confidence to believe she would make her plan work.

As she passed close to the house, she heard children singing and paused to listen. It sounded like they were singing hymns. Their sweet voices filled the evening air with the sound of gratitude. Jennie took a deep breath, realizing it was the first time in a long time that she had felt the stirring of hope.

Chapter 11

For the next several days, Jennie did little else besides making peanut brittle. Every morning, she waited for her husband and children to go their respective ways, then dashed into the kitchen to assemble the ingredients and start experimenting. There were so many variations, and she wanted to find a second tempting version to sell along with the regular peanut brittle. She tried coconut brittle, brittle dipped in chocolate, brittle with almonds and walnuts, and a slew of other combinations. The Fisher family had a steady supply, and realizing that Jennie took their reviews seriously, they made an effort to give her detailed impressions. In the end, she decided the winner was brittle with cashews. She would start by selling that along with the basic peanut brittle and see what developed.

Miraculously, it seemed to Jennie, Mattie's uncle gave his permission to add her candy to his stand. Now all she had to do was come up with a way to package it. She had picked up some small cellophane bags, but they weren't too exciting. Tins would preserve it longer, though preservation wasn't necessary if it was being sold in small quantities that would probably be eaten quickly. She was mulling over the situation as she poured out the contents of a fresh batch, knowing she could start selling it the next day if she could decide on the display.

The front door opened, and her daughter called out to see if anyone was home. Jennie froze. She had lost track of the time, and Willa was back from school. When she entered the kitchen, she regarded the scene with puzzlement. Her mother stood over three baking sheets full of candy, surrounded by dirty dishes and pots, stacks of colorful tins, and assorted utensils.

"It smells so good. What's going on?" Willa came closer. "Is it peanut brittle again? Wow, you sure made a lot."

Even though she had planned on waiting until things were a lot further under way, Jennie decided it couldn't hurt to tell Willa now. Setting down the pot on the stove, she started to explain. Her daughter stared at her in amazement.

"I'm hoping to start the actual selling tomorrow," Jennie concluded, "but I don't have a good idea for packaging. I need a way to display it that will attract some attention."

Willa sat down in a chair, taking everything in. "I can't believe you, Mom. You're starting a business, like, for real."

She laughed. "Well, I'm trying. We could use the money, as you might have guessed."

Willa gave her a look. "*Scout* has probably guessed. Really, Mom, we're not total idiots."

Jennie felt foolish, realizing that she treated her children as if they were small and innocent. They knew everything going on around them. She had, too, when she was their age. So why did she assume they were any different?

"Okay." She sat down across from her daughter. "Then let's work together. Help me come up with a way to make my stuff call out, 'Buy me immediately!'"

Willa closed her eyes, thinking aloud. "Homemade peanut brittle. Fresh, local. Small batches. Special. Not mass-produced." She looked at her mother. "Do you have anything at all to put them in?"

Jennie jumped up to show her the bags and metal tins. "They're fine, just sort of boring."

Willa took a few of each and said she would be back. Intrigued, Jennie cleaned up as she waited. Half an hour later, Willa came downstairs, asking for a few pieces of candy. She turned so her mother couldn't see her, made some adjustments, then turned back and extended the cellophane bag.

The bag was tied with three uneven lengths of different-colored raffia string. Dangling from the knot was a hand-torn tag. Willa had written *Got To Candy* in black ink, using a thin, spidery script above a tiny illustration of two women talking. A cartoon bubble above one head read, *You've got to try this. Simply got to!* The effect was sweet and whimsical.

Jennie looked at her daughter in surprise. "What on earth? I didn't know you could draw like this! Look at these women— they're sophisticated but funny at the same time. I love this!"

"They're just the way I doodle." Though Willa grinned at the praise, her expression turned anxious almost at once. "I want it to say that this is individual, unique, you know, so all of them would have to be hand-done. It's not supposed to look perfect."

Jennie was nodding. "I get that, absolutely." She laughed. "I don't think doing them by hand is a problem, since we're not exactly inundated with orders. You'd have to do the drawings while I tied and attached stuff."

"Could I? That would be so cool. I'd do each one in a different color ink."

"I had no idea we had a marketing executive in the house," Jennie said, shaking her head in wonder. "You have a whole image for this in your head."

"Not for the tins, though. I want to work on those some more. Could you buy solid-colored ones?"

"Sure. Hey, take your time. I'd love to see what you come up with." She moved to hug Willa, who didn't resist. "I can't thank you enough, honey. This is so much better than tying it with a little curly ribbon, which is what I would have done."

Her daughter left, talking to herself. "We need something to say what kind it is and list ingredients, maybe on the back of the tag . . . just draw that once and have it be the same on all of them . . ."

Got To Candy. Why not, Jennie thought. You've got to try it. I've got to get this all to work. She didn't know what to make of Willa's newly revealed creativity. If her daughter hadn't interrupted today's cooking session, Jennie might never have found out about it. It proved that all the time she spent in her room wasn't wasted on the computer; she was thinking, drawing, experimenting. Jennie was overcome with pride in her child. Plus, they were going to work on this project together. If nothing else came of it, that was reward enough.

When Tim got home two hours later, he found his mother and sister working on their own little assembly line to create small bags of candy, each looking slightly different from the last. He looked around, noticing there was no sign of dinner in the works.

"Mom? What's going on?" He swiped a piece of peanut brittle, receiving a light smack on the hand from Jennie. "Wait, you're saying I can't have any?"

"Exactly," she answered. "Let me introduce you to Got To Candy, going on sale tomorrow morning."

"Huh?"

Willa glanced over at him with disgust. "What word didn't you understand, genius? Mom's going to sell this. She's an entrepreneur now."

"Listen to Wilma, using the big words," he said in mock admiration.

"Don't call me Wilma!"

"Whatever. Is there going to be any dinner?"

Jennie hadn't given it any thought. "Sure, in a bit. I'll come up with something."

"Who's going to buy this stuff?" he asked, turning to go. "You're both crazy."

"Thanks for the encouragement," his sister snapped.

"It's okay," Jennie said when they were alone. "You can't blame him for being skeptical. I would be, too. It's not like he ever saw me doing anything like this before."

Besides, she added silently, he only voiced what I've been thinking myself. Maybe tons of peanut brittle was already for sale at the marketplace, and it was better. Or maybe there was too much peanut brittle in the world to allow for one more bite. She didn't know how long she would be allowed to offer her product at the booth if it didn't sell.

As if she had read her mother's mind, Willa said, "Listen, Mom, don't worry. It's going to be awesome."

Jennie looked at her daughter. Such an unlikely source for so much support. Not to mention her truly valuable contributions. Jennie leaned over and planted a kiss on Willa's cheek. "Awesome like you."

"Oh my gosh, Mom, you are so embarrassing."

"It's my job."

"No, this is your job, so get back to work."

They continued with their tasks, smiling.

By the time Shep got home that night, the filled and labeled cellophane bags were neatly displayed in a large basket on the kitchen counter. He came in to get a beer from the refrigerator as Jennie was warming up his dinner in the microwave.

"What's this?" He frowned.

She had been preparing for the moment, but she wasn't looking forward to it. Still, the time had come.

"We're so lucky, Shep," she started out in her most cheerful voice. "Mattie is going to offer these at the marketplace. You know, she's working at one of the booths. So I make them, and she does the selling, and we make money."

"What are you talking about?" He opened a can of beer and took a long drink.

"I'm making this candy to sell." She hated how she sounded, her voice getting higher and higher, like that of some deranged preschool teacher. "It'll be great for us and the Fishers as well. And we could really do well when tourist season arrives."

About to take another drink from the can, he stopped. "Are you saying this isn't a onetime thing? You're going to do this on a regular basis?"

"Yes. Isn't it great?" She heard desperation creeping into her tone.

He picked up one of the bags, reading the label. "Who's 'Got To Candy'?"

"Well . . . me."

His eyes met hers. "You're trying to start a business."

She struggled not to look away. "Yes."

"Even though you know how I feel about you working."

"Shep, this is ridiculous." The words came rushing out of her. "We have to make more money. Have to. I've gone along with this thing you have about your wife not working for all this time, but I'm done with it. It's not a choice for us. Your wife has to work, and this is what I came up with."

He slammed the beer can down on the counter. "Because I can't support us?"

Frustration got the better of her. "Well, yes! I don't blame you. Things are hard for everyone. But we can't live on what that shop brings in, no matter how much we want to pretend we can."

"The store is doing better. Word's gotten out that it's open again, and people are coming back."

"That's news to me."

"It's true. I've been developing my own customers who trust me. Regulars. And the place looks better. I've cleaned it up a lot. Anyway, you can't work because the kids need you to—"

"The kids are in school all day. They don't need me to do anything anymore. Besides, this is flexible, and if they do need me, it won't be a problem."

"You've thought this all out, haven't you? Without discussing it with me."

"I knew what you'd say. What you're saying now. What you've always said."

"I have my reasons."

She exploded. "Maybe you do, but they're not good enough."

He stared at her.

"Look," she said, trying to calm down, "I don't want to do anything to hurt you or make you feel bad in any way. But we need more money. I'm trying to find a way to get some. That's all."

"What makes you think this stuff"—he gestured at the basket's contents—"is going to bring in any real money?"

She just looked at him. "You know," she said quietly, "you haven't even asked to taste it."

He turned and left without another word. Fuming, she went upstairs. Couples were supposed to help each other accomplish things, not throw up unreasonable barriers. He wouldn't let her help with the bike shop, and now he wanted to stop her from doing something constructive for the family. Yes, he was tied to the idea of being the provider, as he had been for his brother when they were young. Mix that with his natural pride, plus the lost years of being the football hero, and you have a deadly combination. He wanted to be the hero, *her* hero, and that was fine, but not if it flew in the face of reality. This was a time for them to work together, like they used to. Instead, he was driving them further apart with his disappointment at himself.

The time for all that was over. Tomorrow morning, she would bring her merchandise to Mattie's booth.

Chapter 12

Jennie pulled up to the Fisher farm just in time to see Mattie climbing into one of the family's buggies. She waved as she took up the reins. Jennie grabbed the basket of peanut brittle and rushed over.

"Do you always leave this early?" she asked. "I thought you'd still be having breakfast."

"There is a lot to do today," Mattie said. "Are you bringing something else for us to taste?"

Jennie grinned, holding up the basket. "Fifty bags. Ready to sell."

Mattie reached out to take it, observing the neat rows of candy. "It looks very nice. I can put it right on the counter." Smiling, she set it on the buggy's floor beside her, then took the reins in both hands again. "Now we will see." She clicked her tongue, and the horse started walking.

"Let me know if you sell any," Jennie called out, immediately feeling foolish. Obviously, Mattie would let her know. There was no point in being so anxious. She had to give it a chance. It could be a week before she made a sale. If she ever did.

The day seemed endless, but late in the afternoon, she answered a knock at the door to find Joshua Fisher standing outside.

"My mother wanted me to tell you that they sold thirty bags of peanut brittle. Can you make more for tomorrow?"

"For tomorrow?" Jennie echoed, too surprised to say anything else.

He nodded.

"Yes, yes, of course." Jennie found her voice, and a wide smile broke across her face. "Please tell her I'll have it to her first thing in the morning."

She watched Joshua walk down the driveway to the road, her mind trying to register what she had just heard. Thirty sales! She whirled around in excitement and slammed the door. "Willa! Honey, get down here!"

"What?" The annoyed tone floated downstairs.

Jennie hurried toward the stairs and called up. "We sold thirty bags! At the market today!"

There was a pause, then the sound of Willa's feet hitting the floor. She came tearing out of her room, practically flying down the steps. "Are you kidding?"

Jennie shook her head. "Can you believe it?"

Her daughter did a few quick dance moves to express her delight, and they hugged.

"We need to replace them for tomorrow."

"Oh, wow. I have to do more labels."

"Okay." Jennie started thinking aloud. "We have to be organized about this. You finish your homework while I make more brittle. Then we'll put the packages together. Will you be okay if we have dinner a little later than usual?"

"Are you kidding? This is huge, Mom!" Willa put up her hand for a high five, which Jennie happily supplied. "You did it, you actually did it. You are truly the bomb-dot-com!"

Jennie had no idea what that meant. "Why, thank you," she said with exaggerated modesty. "But no, we did it together. Definitely, it wouldn't have been the same without your adorable packages."

Willa was already racing back toward her room, anxious to get on with the next batch. Humming, Jennie went back into the kitchen. It wasn't the building of an empire, she thought, but it was something.

Producing the new order kept her and Willa up late that night. When she was finally able to sit down and draw the labels, Willa had to speed up, which resulted in lines that wavered more. It was an unintended improvement, in Jennie's opinion. Still, if they were going to refill the big basket frequently, they would need a more efficient process. As they assembled the bags, they came up with the idea to have Willa draw twenty master labels, each one with a different sketch having one person or animal telling another to try the candy.

Their excitement was almost palpable when Shep arrived home and entered the kitchen. They both greeted him cheerfully but continued measuring and tying the colorful strands of raffia. His face darkened as he watched them, but he merely microwaved the plate of food Jennie had set aside for him, grabbed a beer, and went off to the living room to eat in front of the television. Jennie watched him with a mixture of annoyance and sadness.

Pushing the feelings away, she turned to her daughter. "Hey, what do you say we go over to the market on Saturday and spy on our candy? You know, see what makes people choose it, if they eat it right there or save it, that kind of stuff."

"Totally, yes, let's do it."

Jennie couldn't remember the last time she had seen Willa so excited about anything. When Saturday morning arrived, they brought a new basket filled with fresh candy to the booth, then told Mattie they would hang around to see what happened. Amused, she supplied them each with a doughnut and wished them luck. They moved around as if shopping at the surrounding booths, drifting closer whenever a customer approached Mattie. At first no one seemed interested in the peanut brittle, but suddenly, people started to pick up the little bags at a brisk clip. Jennie and Willa were thrilled every time. Around noon, a man and a woman stopped to buy some pies, and the woman grabbed a bag to add to their order. As her husband was paying, they could see her reading the label, and a smile flickered across her face. She untied the bag and popped a piece into her mouth. As her husband picked up their bread and walked away, she called out after him, "Hon, you've got to try this. It's delicious."

Jennie and Willa stared at each other, then burst out laughing. "She actually said it!" Willa said. " 'You've got to try this!' "

"Do you think she knew we were watching? Was she trying to be funny because she read the label?"

"Whatever it was, it worked."

They approached Mattie to tell her they had seen enough and were leaving.

"We are going to sell them all before the end of the day," Mattie said. "Can you bring back another hundred bags? Half cashew, half peanut—I don't know yet what people will want more."

Jennie was thrilled, but at the same time, she knew she would have to come up with some way to produce brittle more quickly. Unfortunately, that meant hiring someone to help, and she hadn't made anywhere near enough money to afford that—she wasn't even covering the cost of ingredients yet. Well, she thought, in the meantime, she would have to turn to the least likely source of help: her son. Like it or not, he was about to be recruited into the new family candy business.

It was later that afternoon when she next saw Tim. She was vacuuming in the living room while waiting for new batches of brittle to cool, and she happened to glance out the window to see him slowly riding his bicycle up the street, with Peter Fisher beside him on Rollerblades. Both boys looked serious, and when they reached the edge of the driveway, they stopped to continue their discussion. It seemed to Jennie that Peter was upset about something, and Tim was offering advice or perhaps words of comfort. Peter had good reason to be upset, considering he had lost his father. He was also in an odd position, she realized, being the de facto head of the household, yet under the authority of the uncle who had moved into the house for an undetermined amount of time. She couldn't guess what all this was like for the boy or where it was heading. He was only sixteen. Could he wait and take over the farm later? Farming was so important to the Amish, even though many of them could no longer afford to own farms in this area, where land had become so expensive. It was hard to believe the Fishers would want to let go of theirs. It must be a complicated situation for them, she thought, although they never spoke of it.

Peter skated off at high speed, and Tim came inside. She turned off the vacuum cleaner. "Hi. I see Peter was with you. Surprising he has any time off on a Saturday."

"He had to go buy something, if you really want to know. In fact, he said Dad was over there working with his uncle."

"Everything okay with Peter?"

"Sure." He eyed his mother suspiciously. "Why?"

"No reason." She paused. "I'm a little confused about why he spends so much time with you. I mean, I know you're wonderful, but doesn't he have Amish friends?"

"Of course he does," Tim snapped. "He's usually with his own group. Sometimes he just likes to spend time with someone different."

"Does he date anyone?"

He looked exasperated at having to explain himself. "There's a girl he's been hanging out with."

"'Hanging out' is a strange expression for Amish teenagers."

"They go to these things on Sunday nights, I think they're called sings. The boys and girls sing and spend time together. Now that they're older, there's more stuff they can do on the weekends."

"Is he interested in your world?"

"What's with the interrogation?" He was getting visibly annoyed. "It's not *my* world. It's *the* world. He can see it for himself!"

"Sorry." She held up her hands in supplication. "But his dad died, and he's at that age where he might be trying out stuff that isn't really the way the Amish live. I wonder if he isn't looking to you—"

"Why do you have to stick your nose in other people's business all the time?" he interrupted.

She stood up straighter. "Don't speak to me like that."

"You're always asking us about stupid things, trying to get to the way we *feel* about stuff."

"Sorry for caring." The sarcastic words slipped out before she could stop them.

"I'm not so sure if you really do care." His voice was rising in anger. "You chatter away all the time, trying to distract everyone with nonsense when they're actually trying to show what they feel. But you don't ever *do* anything. Nobody ever deals with anything around here. Everybody just walks around mad."

Stung, she stared at him. "You're not sure I care? How could you say that to me?"

"It's easy! If you did care, why did you start this business thing when you know it makes Dad crazy? You're the parent, the one who's supposed to fix things. But you're making them worse!"

"We need more money, Tim. What would you have me do, just sit around?" She didn't want to drag him into their financial problems, but she wasn't going to allow him to criticize her without understanding the situation.

"I don't know!" His words exploded, and she could see the shine of tears in his eyes. "I just want you to fix things!"

"Oh, sweetheart . . ." He was too young to handle this. Even though he was always so mad at Shep, he was trying to protect his father. It hurt him to see his parents so unhappy, and he wanted the pain to go away. That was all he understood.

"We're all doing our best. I'm trying to work things out the best way I know how."

"Yeah, well, it's not good enough!"

As he stormed off, her heart broke for him, but she reminded herself that he would feel a lot worse if they got any deeper into financial trouble. The damage of her attempt to earn money on her own had been done. What remained was the earning of the money. She would have to force herself to focus on that before anything else. The one thing she did understand was that she wouldn't be able to ask Tim for assistance anytime soon.

As she assembled more bags of candy, she went over the question of how to turn the brittle sales into money more quickly. She made a good profit on what she sold, but it was a tiny amount that went right back into the costs. The solution was to increase the volume they sold. But the only way they could do that was to hire more help.

Unless she branched out. Found something else to sell that was less expensive to produce and could be made in bigger batches. She went back to her candy recipe books and started flipping through. Peanut brittle had seemed like the easiest thing to make. She hoped one day she could make sophisticated chocolate creations that justified a higher price, but they weren't an option right now.

Scout came to sit by her, and she leaned over to stroke his back as she read.

"Where is it?" she asked him. "Where is my brainstorm?"

Then she saw it. Lollipops. She had to buy some plastic molds and the sticks. Once she melted a few ingredients and poured the mixture into a mold, that was it. Pop them out, wrap them up. The trick would be to make them special somehow.

"I need my consultant," she told Scout. She went to the bottom of the stairs. "Willa, could you please come down here for a business meeting."

Her daughter appeared, holding a purple pen and a sketchpad, on which she was designing her twenty master sketches for labels. "What's up?"

"New idea. Tell me what you think of this." Jennie explained what she had in mind.

"The key is in the package, like before," Willa said.

Her mother nodded. "One lollipop is like another, really, so it needs to be a fun purchase. They can be generous-sized, but still . . ."

They tossed out different ideas, eventually deciding that

each color lollipop would have a matching color cellophane bag tied over it with the same color raffia and label. This time the label would be a miniature colored translucent envelope with the company name on the outside. Inside each envelope would be one message in Willa's spidery script, reading *I am your lollipop and I love you for buying me* above the ingredient listing, and a second with a fortune or a saying.

"It'll take us a while, but once we get enough fortunes printed, we can just rotate them through batches for several months. We'll see how that goes later," Jennie said. "But I like this. It's friendly. The fortunes should be fun or offbeat." She thought about it. " 'You're sweet, like me,' or 'You could do something to make someone happy—if you want to.' Or some such thing."

"We can't just keep writing the Got To name," Willa reflected. "You need a logo. So people recognize that it's your candy right away."

Jennie stared at her. "You continue to amaze me. I hadn't thought of that."

"Leave it to me."

Over the next few weeks, Jennie and Willa found themselves up late every night producing fresh baskets of brittle and lollipops. They developed a routine: Willa did her schoolwork while Jennie prepared dinner. Then they devoted the rest of the afternoon and evening to Got To Candy. When Tim got home, the three of them ate together, Jennie fruitlessly trying to engage him in some discussion of his day. Eventually, she would give up, and he would eat hurriedly as she and Willa

discussed their business. The two of them invariably didn't finish the next day's order until late at night, when they would fall
into bed, exhausted. Shep neither interfered nor asked anything about what was going on. If she'd had the energy, Jennie
would have tried to discuss the situation with him, but she
knew her fatigue would quickly result in an argument.

In the meantime, sales continued to grow. The warmer
months brought the tourists in full force, and the baskets were
quickly emptied of their contents, replaced several times a day.
Willa had also packaged brittle in larger tins of bright Easter-
egg colors, with the hand-torn label glued onto the sides and
three flat bows attached to the top. Jennie came up with boxes
of two dozen lollipops in assorted colors. They scoured the In-
ternet to find cheap sources for materials. As the summer pro-
gressed, profits started to edge out expenses.

"Our only problem," Willa told her mother as they sat wrapping lollipops one evening, "is that we're going to keel over
from being so tired. Not that I'm complaining, but, like, we
have no life anymore, for real."

And, like, I have no marriage anymore, Jennie thought. For
real. And, like, I have no relationship with my son anymore,
either.

Tim had wanted her to fix things. She had strengthened her
relationship with her daughter, but that had never really been
a problem to begin with. She hadn't helped anybody else get
along, and she had allowed the distance between Shep and her
to widen until they might as well be standing on different con-

tinents. She wondered if she was using their need for money as a distraction from other troubles. But what was more urgent? Did she have to choose one over the other? All she knew for sure was that no matter what choice she made, it would be the wrong one.

Chapter 13

The breezy July Sunday was perfect for a picnic, the sky a dazzling blue. Out in the backyard, Jennie set a tray laden with condiments on the wooden picnic table. Shep had built the table last summer, she recalled, which, incredibly, meant an entire year had passed since they had moved here.

This was the first time she had invited the entire Fisher family over to their house, and they would be bringing Abraham's brother and his relatives as well. Jennie estimated the number of guests to be around twenty-three. The Amish went to church only every other Sunday, and this was one of the days when they wouldn't be attending worship, so they could take time off to visit. Shep was in charge of barbecuing hamburgers and hot dogs, and she had prepared three enormous bowls of potato salad and another three of fruit salad. Going back into the kitchen, she went over a mental list of everything else she would be serving. She tried not to worry about how the Fishers might judge her house—if it was too small, too messy, too *something* not right—and reprimanded herself for worrying, knowing how loath the Amish were to judge other people.

Enlisting her children to set out all the chairs and blankets, she realized it was nearly time for everyone to arrive. She went outside through the front door to make sure Willa had swept the entranceway, as asked, and was greeted by the sight of her guests turning the corner to walk up the road. She stopped, mesmerized by the picture they created. The women and girls were in dresses of maroon, dark green, blue, and gray beneath black aprons, the thin strings of their white kapps trailing down past their shoulders. The men all wore black pants and suspenders across short-sleeve shirts in the same shades as their wives' dresses, and most had on straw hats with narrow black bands. She had seen Efraim but never had the chance to speak to him. From this distance, his resemblance to his late brother was especially jarring; if she hadn't known better, Jennie would swear it was Abraham himself. If only, she couldn't help thinking as a pang of sorrow shot through her. She pushed away the feeling; her intention was to bring a little joy to Mattie's day, not point out sad reminders. Efraim had brought his grown son who had come with his wife and children. She counted three men in the group and wasn't clear on who was who.

Many of the small children were holding hands. Two of the older girls held babies in their arms, while several others carried coolers and baskets of food. The uniformity of their neat and unadorned clothing made them look pristine as they chatted with one another, calmly making their way.

She called for Shep and the children. Everyone met up at the front door, and introductions were made among the children. Shep already knew Abraham's brother, having spent time with him helping out at the farm. Efraim accepted Jennie's words of condolence with a simple nod. His wife, Barbara, was a heavyset woman with dark hair and a stern expression. Jennie had met her several times before, and she was always polite but not much more. Perhaps, Jennie thought, she didn't approve of the family fraternizing with the English. It was understandable. Jennie resolved to do her best to get the woman to overcome her misgivings. On occasion at the Fisher house, Jennie had heard Barbara direct the people around her in no uncertain terms, so she didn't expect to revise her own mental image of the woman as a bit scary. But hey, she thought, if Barbara wanted to organize everyone today to get things accomplished, she was welcome to do so.

The mystery guest turned out to be Barbara's brother Zeke, a widower who lived some sixty miles away and had come to meet his sister to go over some legal papers about family property elsewhere. Jennie didn't follow the story entirely, but she took an instant liking to the man, whose friendliness provided a notable contrast to his sister's reserve.

Efraim and Barbara's son Red was married to a woman named Ellen, whose innate sweetness was instantly apparent. Jennie guessed that she was only twenty-five or so, but they already had six young children. They had taken the time to help Mattie before continuing on their journey to a new home in Ohio. At last the introductions were completed, and everyone was accounted for. The men took most of the children around back, while Jennie marveled at the food the Fisher women were briskly adding to the already full table: chowchow, macaroni salad, pickles, four large thermoses of lemonade and root beer, a huge basket full of homemade breads and muffins, and an enormous platter of chicken.

"There was no need for you to bring all this," Jennie said to Mattie.

"We wanted to," she replied. "We are so many people to feed."

"You were just worried you wouldn't get enough to eat," Jennie teased.

The other woman laughed.

"At least I can promise no peanut brittle today. You must be sick of the sight of it."

"If peanut brittle is helping your family, I am happy to look at it as often as you like."

Jennie regarded her friend with affection as they joined the others. Once everyone had loaded up their plates with food, the entire group said a silent grace.

The barbecue grew lively. Children jumped up to play games or explore the unfamiliar setting. Jennie watched them become intrigued or amused by flowers, bugs, rocks, and whatever else they found at hand. Scout was thrilled by the attention he got, as the children petted him and threw a tennis ball for him to retrieve; with so many children, he was able to play his favorite game until he grew exhausted, an opportunity he rarely got when Jennie was tossing the ball. The girls played clapping games. There were excited voices and laughter, but no arguments or childish squabbling. No need for video games or cell phones here, she thought. Although Tim and Peter immediately gravitated toward each other, they participated in various activities with the smaller children. Jennie was delighted to see her son smiling as he tossed a ball with the young Fisher cousins. Such a rare occurrence these days, she reflected.

She was also pleased to note Shep talking easily to Efraim while he flipped burgers at the grill. Most satisfying to her was the sight of Willa sitting with Nan. At long last, her daughter was making an effort. They were joined by Ellen Fisher. The three began an animated conversation, Willa doing most of the talking. Jennie could only guess that her daughter was explaining their candymaking. Sure enough, when she passed by, Willa waved her over to listen in.

"Mom, hey," she said, "Ellen had a suggestion. Nan and she can package stuff for us."

Jennie smiled at her daughter. "That's a great idea, honey, but you know we can't pay anyone yet." She looked at Ellen. "If only we could, I would jump at the offer."

"I understand," Ellen said, "but Mattie told me you're doing very well at the booth. She said you just need to get some help. We could start now, and you can pay us later, when you have enough."

Jennie stared at her in surprise. "I don't know what to say."

"Please just say yes."

"That's a very kind offer, but you barely know me. You're taking a big risk."

"You are Mattie's friend. That is all I need to know. Also, you would be helping me, too. I have found some work cleaning at a hotel, but not enough. This will be a good situation."

"Okay, then. Fantastic," Jennie said.

Ellen nodded. "It's settled. We can work out the details later."

Jennie stood there, marveling at her good fortune. It was all a result of having met the Fishers, she mused. If not for the example Mattie had set, Jennie never would have taken action to solve their financial problems. Then the Fishers' generosity had provided a place to sell what she made. Now they were stepping in again, giving her another leg up with people to help whose payment she could postpone. Mattie had done all this while caring for her huge family alone, her husband snatched from her side. Jennie realized she could never again say it was too difficult to get something done, not after seeing what this woman was capable of.

"Mom," Tim said, coming up behind her, "Peter and some of his friends are going to take me fishing with them, okay?"

She hesitated. "I guess so . . ."

"Come on, this is almost over. I won't be back late."

"Okay, but remember—"

He was already out of earshot, hurrying off. She supposed she should be grateful he had stayed around this long. Plus, now that she thought about it, he and Shep hadn't exchanged a cross word this afternoon, at least not in front of her or their company. That was something, wasn't it? Not really, she corrected herself; refraining from getting into a squabble during an enjoyable barbecue was hardly a major accomplishment. Besides, she hadn't done anything to fix the problems bubbling beneath the surface.

At the sound of her name, she turned to find Mattie calling. She stood with her out-of-town guest, Barbara Fisher's brother Zeke. Jennie went over, asking if they needed anything.

"I wanted to say that I appreciate being included in your picnic today," Zeke said. "It's a good afternoon here."

Jennie was used to the Amish tendency toward understatement and delighted by the compliment. "Have you come from very far?" she asked him, wondering how he had managed to get away during what she knew was a busy part of the farming season.

"Sixty miles."

"Do you farm?"

He shook his head. "I'd like to, but I build furniture in a factory. Two of my brothers have farms, and I worked with them for a long time. There's one that I'm thinking about buying on my own, and I'm almost ready to do it."

"Is Barbara your younger or older sister?"

"Bossy Barbara? She's older." He laughed. Jennie was taken aback that he would make such a joke, but Mattie smiled. Apparently, Jennie had guessed right about Barbara's personality, and it was no secret to anyone. It dawned on her that she had assumed the Amish were all as sweet and loving as Mattie all the time. They were just people, like everyone else. They had their good and bad points and their personal ups and downs.

The three continued chatting for a bit, then Jennie walked over to Shep, who was scraping off the grill.

"Awesome job, honey," she told him. "My cheeseburger was great."

She saw with discomfort that he was genuinely startled to get a compliment from her. When had things gotten this bad between them?

"Thanks. You did great yourself. And they're still here, so I guess it's a successful get-together," he said.

They stood there, looking into each other's eyes. He nodded and smiled. It felt good, she thought, like being wrapped in a warm quilt.

Willa appeared beside them. "I'm going to take Nan and Ellen inside to show them how we do our packages," she told her mother, excitement evident in her voice.

The reference to the candy business immediately severed the connection between Jennie and Shep. He turned away, directing his full attention back to the grill. She gave a small sigh.

"Sure, Willa," she said, suddenly exhausted. "Sure thing."

The next night, the two of them drove over to the farm with cartons of candy and packaging supplies. Ellen and Nan helped them unload the car, and they all sat down at the kitchen table to go over the steps. As usual, the house was dimly lit but cozy and filled with activity. At a folding table with a large bowl of popcorn in the middle, several children worked on a jigsaw puzzle together, and others were busy with an art project. Becky played with the dollhouse.

Ellen's husband, Red, came in to greet Jennie. He was giving a laughing toddler a ride on his shoulders, and Jennie reached up to tickle the little boy's neck as Red thanked her again for the barbecue.

"And now you and my wife will work together," he said. "Very good."

"Let's go to work," Ellen said, joining Willa and Nan at the table, where they were already deep in conversation about the finer points of raffia.

Jennie was on her way to take a seat when she happened to notice two of the children at the table using rubber stamps to create designs on a large piece of white paper. She paused. "Willa," she said, "can you come here?"

Her daughter moved to stand beside her. "What?"

She gestured toward the artwork. "How would you feel about rubber-stamping some of the labels? It's more personal than something printed by machine, because it's imperfect, but you don't have to draw it yourself, so it's faster."

The girl's face lit up. "Genius, Mom."

"Different color inks."

"Of course."

They looked at each other in delight.

"Mom," Willa announced, "you are rocking this candy thing in every way!"

They hadn't heard Mattie come into the room, but she was beside them.

"How fast can you get a rubber stamp?" she teased. "Because my cousins told me they ran out of your candy again yesterday two hours before closing. The lollipops were gone by three o'clock."

"I don't believe this." Jennie was shocked. "Who would have expected . . . ?"

"It's a good thing you've got your helpers here," Mattie said, gesturing to Nan and Ellen, "because you should make twice as much brittle from now on and more of it in the tins. People like it and come back to buy in bigger quantities. I have had some people go away very unhappy when we had none left."

"Soon the booth itself won't be big enough to sell it," Ellen said in amusement, setting out the fortunes for the lollipops by color.

Jennie wondered if that could be true, if there might come a day when she would have to find another outlet. She would sell the candy through the Fishers' booth for as long as they would have her, but maybe she should also sell it in some other places.

A sense of fear shot through her. She was reaching too far, too fast. She didn't know what she was doing, she thought, when you got right down to it. Expanding might prove to be the last straw for Shep. It was all going to backfire somehow.

Confused, she covered her eyes with one hand, listening to Willa explaining the details of boxing peanut brittle to her attentive audience. What surprised her was the quiet confidence in her daughter's tone, a confidence Jennie had never heard. She looked over at Willa, realizing something wonderful had taken place, and it was all because of their collaboration on the candy. It occurred to her that this alone was reason enough to continue.

Chapter 14

Jennie answered the telephone to hear a delighted greeting from the person on the other end.

"Michael?" she asked. "Is that you?"

"Hey, it's been too long," he said. "How are you, J?"

"Great, great."

She didn't know if Shep and his brother had been in much contact over the seven months since their families' disappointing Christmas dinner together. After that night, she had written him a note thanking him for the gift of money, but they hadn't had an occasion to talk since.

"How are Lydia and the kids?" she asked.

"We're all good. What I want to know is how you guys are making out."

He sounded genuinely interested. She wondered what had prompted this after so much seeming indifference.

"Everybody's finding their way," she said, hoping that sounded positive.

"What about you, you personally?"

"Actually, I'm doing this little thing with Willa. We're making and selling candy. Our own mini-empire." She laughed.

"That's what Shep told me. Sounds like it's going gangbusters. He's super-proud of you."

She was speechless. Not only had her husband told his brother about her work, but he'd actually said he was proud of her? Impossible. He hadn't said a single word to her about the business since their initial argument. As far as she could tell, he was pretending it wasn't happening. Yet according to Michael, Shep was watching everything and feeling good about what she was doing.

"So I have to taste some of what you're selling," her brother-in-law was saying. "Can I order it online?"

"Online?" She laughed. "Honestly, Michael, we're not really a big company. We sell at the market here."

"You don't have to be big to sell online. In fact, that's how you *get* big."

"Oh, come on. That's a whole other thing."

"No, it isn't. You set up a website. No big deal. Then you get your name out there."

"I hadn't considered it, I guess."

"Go look at websites from other companies and see what kind you like. Then get a professional to design one for you. You want me to get you some names?"

She smiled. He didn't know about her secret weapon, Willa. Her daughter could come up with the ideas for it, and they would get someone to translate them into a site. "Maybe later, thanks, but I'm going to follow your advice. I really appreciate it." She paused, lowering her voice in case anyone else in the house was nearby. "Just like I really appreciate everything you've done for me. That mon—"

He jumped in. "Me? I haven't done anything. So, is my brother around?"

"I'll get him."

She put down the phone, thinking how much she loved Michael, wishing he were back in their lives the way he used to be. Sticking her head into the living room, she found Shep sitting on the couch, reading a manual, and told him his brother was on the phone. As he got up, she looked at him with fresh eyes. He caught her staring and tilted his head.

"What?"

"Oh . . . nothing."

She wished she knew what to say. That she loved him and was sorry for the terrible words and silences that had passed between them. That he was a better man than she had been giving him credit for. The opportunity was lost as her husband walked by.

She went upstairs to Willa's room. Pausing outside the door, she heard her daughter's voice, apparently in the middle of a one-sided conversation. She knocked, and there was a delay before an irritated command to come in. Jennie found her on the bed, shutting the cover of her laptop.

"I thought you were on the phone," she said to Willa.

"I was talking to a kid in my class. On the computer," she added in response to Jennie's puzzled look. "Mom, you are so out of it. No one talks on the phone, ever."

"Oh, right. What was I thinking? A kid in your class . . ."

"Yeah, a friend."

Jennie almost held her breath. Willa hadn't said a word about making any friends at school, not once in all this time.

"From last term? Will this person be starting high school with you next month?"

"*This person*, as you so weirdly put it, is a girl, and yes, she'll be in school with me. We kinda got friendly toward the end of the year, and we've been video-chatting."

Jennie decided to leave the subject alone, guessing that even one more question would be perceived as prying, and Willa would shut down. "I just got off the phone with Uncle Michael."

Sitting on the edge of the bed, she told Willa about his suggestion to sell their candy online. By the time she left the room, her daughter was back on her computer, looking at food websites.

"I *have* to finish that logo design. Need that first . . ." she was muttering to herself as Jennie shut the door. "You realize we're going to have to sell more types of candy!" she called out.

A mini-mogul at thirteen, Jennie thought with a smile. About to turn fourteen, though, she reminded herself, in only a few weeks. As she went downstairs, Jennie considered what type of birthday cake to bake. Maybe they would invite this new friend over. The notion that her daughter might have found someone her own age to talk to made Jennie want to weep with joy.

Shep and Tim quickly learned about the plans for a Got To Candy website. It would have been impossible for them not to, considering the time Jennie and Willa spent talking about it, and the sketches and printouts of design ideas lying around the house. Maybe it was seeing his mother and sister helping each other with such obvious enjoyment, but on Friday night, Tim offered to help his father out at the store the next day. His offer was greeted by a shocked silence from the other three members of his family, although Shep recovered quickly enough to accept, and in a casual tone, as if this weren't the last thing he had ever anticipated hearing from his son.

The two set off early the next morning, Shep in the truck, Tim on his bicycle. When Jennie heard her son come back in the house less than two hours later, she sighed, knowing that his early return didn't bode well. His expression told her she was right.

"He's ridiculous!" Tim shouted, yanking open the refrigerator door and grabbing the container of milk. He slammed it down on the counter and grabbed a box of cookies from a cabinet. Then he took both to the kitchen table, where he shoved a cookie into his mouth and took a swig of milk directly from the plastic bottle.

"Don't do that." Jennie reached for a glass to bring him.

"He's the most unreasonable . . ." Tim pounded his fist on the table.

"Calm down," she admonished him. "What on earth happened?"

"He doesn't want to bring that place into the twentieth century, forget the twenty-first century! I told him he needed to sell more stuff and get a website and a lot of other things that seemed super-obvious to me. He got all huffy and insulted, like I thought I knew better than he did. Which I do!"

"Oh, dear," she murmured. "Were there any customers at all?"

"Yeah, plenty," he said in annoyance as he chewed. "But he could have tons more."

She was encouraged to hear about the customers and only wished Shep had wanted to tell her himself that the business had picked up. Then she remembered that he had tried to tell her the day he found out about her candy business. He had said something about developing regular customers, or something along those lines. She hadn't paid attention because they'd been arguing.

Tim was still worked up over his father's reluctance to listen. "You and Wilma are all over this stuff. Why is he so backward?"

"To be fair, I didn't even think of the website myself. It was a suggestion."

"But you took it, instead of being all pigheaded!"

"We're trying to take it. All we have is ideas. I don't have a clue how to implement them."

"What do you mean?" He took another cookie, calming down.

"We're coming up with a way we want it to look in a perfect

world. But we don't know how to set it up, and I doubt I can afford to pay anyone to do it."

He looked at her in surprise. "Mom, I can do it for you. Why didn't you ask me?"

"You? I didn't know you could do something like that."

"It's not hard. If I can't do some pieces of it, I can get another kid at school to help me. There are lots of people who know how to set up websites."

"You have people to ask?" She'd never heard him discussing other kids at school.

"Of course I do." Annoyance flashed across his face. "You think I'm a total loser, don't you?"

"No, no, but it seems like you spend most of your free time with Peter Fisher."

"That's not true. He's a really different kind of kid, so I like him, but hey . . ." He got up, grabbing a handful of cookies to take with him. "Tell me when you're ready, and I'll do the website. Maybe *someone* here will appreciate what I can do."

As she replaced the milk in the refrigerator, she felt both thrilled that Tim could handle the last piece of the website puzzle, as well as unhappy that their last fight had been about her business and that he wanted to help her because he was back to fighting with his father. It also saddened her that Shep hadn't drawn on their son's talents. Tim was growing up, had turned sixteen the previous month, and was old enough to be taken seriously. He had made some suggestions about selling more accessories for serious bikers, and his ideas seemed pretty straightforward, but Shep was refusing help from anyone in any form. Willa also could have been of use to him, and he couldn't have missed seeing that she had a flair for marketing things and enjoyed doing it. Her husband was truly, she thought, the most stubborn man in the world.

It took another three weeks, but the Got To Candy website was at last up and running. Jennie wanted to burst with pride over the work her children had done. Willa's designs were in the same whimsical spirit as the candy labels, and Tim had done a terrific job translating them into bright pastel-colored screens that were charming and easily navigated. He asked a boy from school to take photographs of the candy, which had produced beautiful, appetizing portraits of everything in all different types of packaging. Jennie would have liked to show the site to Mattie but didn't bother to suggest it, unsure if she would be putting her friend in a position where she could be breaking a rule by looking at a computer screen.

The whole situation seemed unreal. The moment when Jennie grasped that it was happening was when she opened the delivery of a thousand business cards, purple ink on white stock. There was Willa's logo design in her spidery script: a hand holding a lollipop, the drawing leading into the company name. Jennie stared at the mailing address, a post office box she had started renting, and the link to their website. Would anybody order anything?

A routine emerged. Every day Jennie made fresh batches of candy that she delivered to the Fishers'. In the afternoons, Willa went over to work on packing the candy with Nan and Ellen. After two hours, she came home to do schoolwork and eat dinner while the Fishers continued. Jennie worked from the house, processing online orders, ordering ingredients and shipping supplies, and trying to generate publicity for Got To Candy. When she was done for the day, Jennie would go over to the farm to hand over the new written orders, sometimes slipping them under the kitchen door if she got there too late to find anyone awake. In the mornings, Mattie took what had been prepared for the market, every package containing a business card so customers could order online. It was exhausting for Willa but even more so for Jennie, who found herself working or thinking about Got To Candy round the clock, every single day.

She could hardly complain. As if out of nowhere, the orders started appearing and never let up. Soon Sarah Fisher had joined her sister and cousin putting together boxes to be shipped. Jennie promised to pay Tim, who now had his driver's license, to take the packages to the post office and ship them every other afternoon. She and Willa agreed that they were, respectively, president and vice president of the company and shouldn't get paid yet. Any profit they made later, Willa told her mother, should be put into a savings account for college. Jennie hugged her daughter and told her that was the perfect plan. She decided her own profits would go into a college fund for Tim.

The day Jennie wrote the first paychecks, to the Fishers and to her son, was one of the happiest days she could remember. She took a special satisfaction when, two weeks later, she paid off the balance to the veterinary hospital for Scout's old medical bill. As she sealed the envelope, she gave it a quick kiss. After all, she thought, smiling at her own silliness, if it hadn't been for that bill, none of this would have happened. She baked a chocolate cake, and that night she and the kids celebrated their freedom from the debt.

The only thing that kept it from being a pure joy was Shep's absence. As usual, he didn't say anything, but she could see the hurt in his eyes. She couldn't help thinking he was unhappy about being left out of all the activity and excitement. Yet he expressed no interest. In fact, she noticed he was spending more of what little free time he had at the Fisher farm, helping Peter, Efraim, and Red. There was so much to do on a farm in the summer, they were always glad to have the extra hands.

It was on a Saturday afternoon that she happened to pass by the living room and see him in the process of taking down his awards. She'd thought he was at the farm, but he had come into the house without her hearing. Standing quietly, she watched him pulling the framed certificates off the walls, then prying out the hooks with a hammer. After piling them up, he took an empty carton and started packing his trophies into it. She couldn't make out what his expression meant. Finally, he glanced up to spot her in the doorway. They stared at each other in silence. Then he went back to what he was doing.

She backed away from the doorway. Those awards had been out and visible since the day they got married. They meant everything to him. They were a part of his identity. Yet he was putting them away, out of sight. Perhaps he felt so bad about himself that he couldn't face them anymore. Tears formed in her eyes. She didn't want him to lose himself because of her fledgling business success. But what she realized was that her little business was somehow becoming a part of *her* identity. And she wasn't ready to put it away now that she had found it.

Chapter 15

"The stitches are much smaller here, yes?" Ellen Fisher pointed to an area on the quilt and held it closer so Naomi, her seven-year-old daughter, could get a better look. She added something in Pennsylvania Dutch that Jennie didn't understand.

Ellen was particularly good at quilting, a skill shared by many Amish women. Jennie had chanced to walk in one day when Ellen, Barbara, and Mattie were seated around the quilting frame, working on this very piece, white with a complicated motif of birds, flowers, and hearts. They explained to her that on some days, a number of women came over and they all worked on it together. It was a magnificent piece of art, in Jennie's opinion. The skill of quilting was taught by mother to daughter, so as soon as Naomi was ready, she would join the others at the table. Jennie loved the continuity of traditions and rituals, the way they were passed down from one generation to the next. She wanted to laugh, thinking about how her own daughter was teaching *her* about the rituals of technology, rituals being developed in the world outside this kitchen. She wasn't sure how to think about what was being gained and what was being lost. Although she was thrilled by the success of their candy business, something in her wished she could stay forever in this kitchen, where the timeless traditions were practiced and respected.

She returned to what she was doing, picking up sealed packages ready to be shipped. Tim was outside putting a batch in the trunk. She realized how ridiculous it was that she hadn't invested in a hand truck; there were too many orders to continue piling them into cartons and carrying those out one at a time. In fact, there would soon be too many to fit into her car. That might mean Tim's dream would come true, and he would be driving his own car or, in this case, a van of some kind. Right now he was borrowing her car all the time, which wasn't an ideal situation, to say the least. Perhaps it was time to investigate different ways of shipping, ones that didn't involve making a trip to the post office. Jennie knew she was lagging behind her own company's growth, but it was hard for her to believe it was so steadily expanding, orders coming in from different parts of the country. Maybe tourists tried her candy at Mattie's booth and then went home and ordered more, or maybe her publicity efforts were paying off, but either way, she could see the day coming when she would need more people and a bigger space in which to cook.

Willa and Nan came into the kitchen, their faces reddened by the first day with an autumn chill in the air. Jennie noted with pleasure that they looked comfortable with each other, the awkwardness of their early encounters gone. Both girls were eating apples from the Fishers' small orchard, half a dozen trees that Mattie tended with great care.

"Um, so crunchy, Mom," Willa greeted her, holding out the half-eaten fruit. "Want a bite?"

She shook her head. "You guys still working or done for the day?"

"We're finished. Everybody's in the barn with the horses. Dad just got here, too."

"My mother and some of my cousins are going to wash the buggies next," Nan said.

"Do you need a ride home?" Jennie asked her daughter.

"No, I'll walk later."

Jennie smiled, pleased that Willa wanted to stay with Nan. At last, she thought gratefully, they had developed a real friendship. Between Nan and the girl at school, Willa had the companionship she needed and, as she put it, all she had time for. Exiting with her arms full of boxes, Jennie deposited everything in the car, then went back toward the barn, spotting Tim talking to Peter over by the chicken coop. She found Mattie, ready with a brush and bucket of soapy water, as her eldest daughter wheeled one of the buggies outside with the assistance of some of her girl cousins. Shep was inside, kneeling down beside Red, the two of them examining one of the horses' hooves. Seeing her, he gave a quick wave. He had brought Scout, who was alternating between barking playfully at the Fishers' dog, the sedately seated Hunter, and sniffing madly around the barn.

"Can I help?" Jennie asked Mattie.

"No need, thank you." All the girls had grabbed brushes and were at work scrubbing.

"Okay, I'll be at my house if anybody's looking for me." She went to her car, calling for Tim, who took large, loping strides across the grass to join her.

"Peter and I are going to hang out tonight," he said, buckling his seat belt. "So can I have the car?"

It was Saturday night, but it wasn't as if she and Shep had any big plans. She couldn't remember the last time they'd had any big plans. "Sure. Do you know what you're going to do?"

He shrugged.

"That sounds like fun." She smiled as she turned the key in the ignition.

The four of them had dinner together that evening, a rare event. Shep and Tim had pretty much given up talking to each other rather than arguing any further. It may have been preferable to shouting, but it hurt Jennie to see; they didn't make a point of it, yet somehow they managed to avoid addressing each other except when absolutely necessary. Willa, though, seemed to have gained a grudging respect in her brother's eyes, and he had abandoned his usual custom of giving her a hard time. Jennie found herself reverting to her habit of filling the uncomfortable quiet with chatter. It was funny, she thought: The Fishers didn't talk much during meals, yet their silences were comfortable and without tension.

After cleaning up, Willa retreated to her room, and Tim went out to meet Peter. Jennie did a quick check of the food supplies for both the house and the business in anticipation of the week ahead, then got into bed with a magazine, amazed by the luxury of having time to read. Within fifteen minutes, she had fallen asleep. The ringing of the telephone woke her up. The room was dark, and Shep was beside her, also awakened by the insistent sound. It must be late at night, she realized.

He picked up the receiver. "Yes?"

There seemed to be a lot of talking on the other end, as he didn't say anything else for a long while, but swung his legs over the side of the bed and sat up. At last he spoke. "Okay, calm down, Tim. Did you call an ambulance? Or the police?"

"*What?*" Jennie bolted up and moved closer to her husband, trying to hear what their son was saying on his end of the phone. "Shep, what is it? Is he all right?"

Shep turned and nodded, mouthing, *He's fine.*

"Why does he need an ambulance?" she asked, frantic.

He held up a finger, indicating to her to wait a moment. "Exactly where are you two?" He got his answer. "We're on our way over. Call for an ambulance, but don't move, either of you, literally, do not move."

"Shep, what's going on?"

"He and Peter got into a car accident. Sounds like Peter got hurt, but I couldn't make out from Tim if it's serious."

Jennie was already out of bed, throwing on a pair of jeans and a T-shirt. The two of them raced out and into Shep's truck.

"It's only a mile and a half from here." He sped out of their driveway.

"What were they doing there?"

"No idea."

They didn't say anything else, and Jennie pointed when she spotted them ahead, illuminated by their headlights. There was her car on the side of the road, the front on the driver's side smashed in, both boys on the ground behind it.

"Ambulance isn't here yet," Shep muttered, pulling off the road and stopping short of the boys.

Jennie jumped out. "Tim, Peter, are you okay?" Tim got up and came over to her. She grabbed him in a hug, and he didn't resist. "Oh, honey, what happened?"

"Why are you walking?" Shep asked in annoyance as he joined them. "You could be injured."

"I'm fine," he said. "Peter's the one who got hurt."

Jennie hurried over and dropped to her knees. Peter was sitting on the ground, bent over, cradling his right arm. He was hurt, yes, but something else about him seemed not right, different somehow. Then it hit her: He wasn't wearing his Amish clothes. The black pants and light short-sleeved shirt and suspenders had been replaced by faded blue jeans and a T-shirt. He looked like he could be any boy who went to school with Tim. It was almost shocking to see him this way. The Amish clothes were an enormous part of who they were. Still, Jennie doubted he could shed his Amish identity just by changing a few garments.

"Where do you hurt?" she asked.

"Just my shoulder," Peter said through clenched teeth.

"Did you call the ambulance?" Shep asked Tim.

"I'm not an idiot," he snapped. "Yes."

"Did you let your mother know?" Jennie asked Peter. "Should my husband or I drive over there?"

"No!"

She was startled by the sharpness of his response. "She has to be told, Peter. The sooner the better."

He shook his head, wincing at the pain it caused him. "It will just worry her. This is my right shoulder, so I won't be able to do any work with it now."

"You don't honestly think that's what she'll be worried about, do you?" Jennie asked.

"No, but she needs to be worried about it. My uncle and everybody were going to leave soon. Now . . ." He dropped his head.

Shep came over and knelt on Peter's other side. "You know it will work out. Besides, it's not like you can hide this. And soon it'll heal, and you'll be ready to run the farm again."

"You don't understand . . ." Peter shut his eyes as his words trailed off.

Tim came to stand beside them. "It's okay," he said to his friend. "You can tell them. It's going to come out now anyway."

Peter raised anguished eyes to Shep. "I don't want to run the farm. I never wanted to. I've been thinking about leaving."

"Leaving? To go where?" Jennie asked.

"I mean leaving our faith."

"Is that what you were doing tonight?" Shep turned to look at Tim. "Were you driving him away somewhere?"

Before he could answer, Peter responded. "No, we were out partying."

Jennie inhaled sharply. "What does that mean?"

"We met up with some kids at a house a few miles down the road." He gestured with his left hand. "It's empty. Being renovated, so nobody's there at night."

"We just wanted a place to hang out, you know," Tim offered, biting his thumbnail.

"A house under renovation is still someone's property," Shep said, "so that would be breaking and entering."

"We weren't doing anything. Just drinking beer and stuff."

There was a momentary silence as the unspoken offense of underage drinking hung in the air.

"And then?" Jennie prompted.

"Some idiot called on his cell phone to order a pizza. So we got out of there. We knew once they saw us in that empty house, the police would come."

"He ordered a pizza," Shep echoed in amazement. "That would be funny if this situation weren't so horrible."

"Go on," Jennie said. "You'd had some beers and decided to drive away. Tim, did you think you should get behind the wheel in that condition?"

"It wasn't Tim," Peter said quietly. "I was driving."

"You?" Jennie was shocked. "Do you even know how?"

"Yes." His voice grew softer. "I don't have a license or anything, but I can drive. Except I guess I had a little too much to drink, because I lost control. The car went off the road, and we hit this rock. It's pretty big, so that was that. The airbags deployed, but somehow I wrenched my shoulder."

"I don't believe this." She got up and brushed herself off, walking a few steps away to make sure she stayed calm.

Her son had been drinking illegally, having a party in someone else's house, then he'd allowed a drunken boy without a license to drive her car. Which had led to this accident. There were about a dozen ways in which she was furious, horrified, and bewildered by his deception and poor judgment. She groaned aloud as another thought hit her: She could never face Mattie again, not after the way Tim had influenced Peter.

As if reading her thoughts, Peter called out to her. "It wasn't Tim's fault. This was my friend's party, and I made him come."

"All that aside, Tim is responsible for my car," she answered.

"Okay, wait a second here." Shep sat down on the ground and looked Peter in the eye. "Let's go back to the other stuff about leaving."

"Yeah. I've been thinking about it for a long time."

"You knew this?" Shep asked his son.

Tim nodded. "We've talked about it a lot."

Shep turned back to Peter. "Makes sense. So, how do you go about making that final decision?"

"It's a terrible decision to make. My mother would be so upset. But she also wouldn't have anyone to run the farm. So I haven't been able to leave." Peter shook his head in misery. "I'm not sure I even want to do it. I don't know."

Shep's tone was respectful. "Would you mind if I asked why you want to leave?"

Peter stared at the ground. "I feel bad telling you." There

was a long pause before he spoke again. "Like I said before, I don't want to farm. We respect farming, and it's a very good thing to have your own farm. But I don't want to do it, and that's the worst thing. And I have no brothers who really help. I used to help my father, and it was a lot of work then, but it was okay. Now he's gone, and there's no one to help me when my uncle leaves."

"It's a lot of responsibility," Shep said.

"Everyone expects me to do it, and I should want to do it. They believe I can manage it all. But I can't!" His tone grew more agitated. "I can't live up to these expectations, to be a farmer and take care of everybody else in the family. I'm not ready, and I may never be ready!"

No one spoke.

"I feel bad about my mother. But it's too soon. I don't know if I want to be baptized. I've always done what I was supposed to do, so they expect me to keep doing it. But it's getting harder without my father, and I'm afraid I'm failing at it. I can't tell anybody. That's not our way, and it would be wrong to worry my mother even more. But what if I wreck the farm? They'll know I failed and have to live with that."

"Wow," Shep said.

Peter looked at him. "You think I'm failing my family?"

"Oh, no, that's not it at all." Shep ran a hand through his hair. He lowered his voice to a whisper, though it was clear that his wife and son were listening. "It's because I hear so much of my own story in yours."

"What do you mean?"

Shep gathered his thoughts. "I played football in high school. I was good at it. But it turned out that was the only thing I was good at. When I got married, I wanted to be a good husband and provider. But I wasn't. I failed at everything I ever tried."

Jennie listened, afraid to breathe. She had never heard her husband talk about his past with anyone. Certainly, she had never heard him explain the way he felt about how things had gone for him when he was no longer the star quarterback.

"The point is," he went on, "that I wanted to run away, like you do. Things weren't working out, and everybody was counting on me. I felt like I had let everyone down, and I continued to do that for years. I couldn't succeed, no matter what I tried. I just wanted things to go back the way they were, like when I played ball. Like you want to go back to when your dad was running the farm. But that doesn't happen. No matter how much we want it."

He was quiet, and everyone waited for what felt like an eternity. At last he spoke again.

"I took it out on my family. I didn't let my wife bail us out because I was too ashamed to let anyone know she might have to be the one to support us. I *sort of* encouraged my son at football, but not nearly as much as I could have, because it caused me so much pain to be around the game. I guess I felt like, if I was a failure in every way, we were all going to be failures. It's only now that I see if I hadn't been such a jerk, if I had only asked for some help along the way, things could have gone very differently."

"Dad . . ." Tim started to speak, then hesitated.

Shep continued to address Peter. "You need to get this out on the table with your mother and your uncle. They should be involved in figuring out how to handle the farm. There isn't a rule that you have to farm, is there? Don't you think something else could be worked out short of you running away? If you choose not to get baptized, that's a different issue, but I hate to see you leave because you're too embarrassed to admit you don't want to run the farm."

"Personal stuff is not something I ever talk about to my parents . . . or did, I mean," Peter said.

"The farm isn't personal stuff," Shep said. "It's the family's business, their livelihood."

Peter nodded slowly, as if to himself. "I've been thinking about it as my private problem. Because I feel as if I've failed."

"Like I did," Shep said. "It's taken me years to see it's not my personal problem. It became everyone's problem, but I didn't let anyone do anything to solve it. Your running away without working it out first is going to create far more problems than it solves."

All four of them turned at the far-off sound of an approaching siren. The ambulance or the police, Jennie thought.

"When the authorities get here, let me talk to them, boys," Shep said, standing up. "We're going to tell the truth, but we'll get through this together."

Tim walked over to stand beside his father. "Thanks, Dad."

Shep looked at him, his son so tall they were eye to eye. "No problem," he said, putting an arm around Tim.

Chapter 16

Jennie and Willa drove on ahead in her car, leaving Shep and Tim to secure the tree in the back of Shep's truck. This year's tree was full and healthy, and Jennie couldn't wait to decorate it. Unpleasant memories of last year's Christmas still chafed enough to justify a small splurge for a nicer one this time around. Besides, she reassured herself, they could afford it. Her business was growing, slowly but steadily, and the holiday should bring them new customers. She and Willa had already started shipping decorated Christmas lollipops. Along with the traditional decorations they had some delicate and unusual ones as well: a patterned mitten, two tiny presents, sparkling tree ornaments. Jennie was proud of their creations and the way they kept edging their designs further into the unusual and humorous. Customers loved the offbeat humor and artwork that came with the sweets. In January, Got To Candy would be offering caramel popcorn, assuming, Jennie thought, that the marketing department—Willa—was ready with a clever idea for the packaging. Eventually, they hoped to offer candies geared to holidays throughout the year, but for now they were happy to have gotten their Christmas pops ready to go in November.

The day was overcast and frigid. Back in the house, Jennie put a kettle of water on the stove to make tea, planning to warm up before she got down to the day's tasks. Today was Sunday, so she had time before Thanksgiving to do advance preparation. It was going to be just the four of them, but it wouldn't have felt right to leave out any of the traditional dishes. By doing some each day, she would prevent getting overwhelmed later in the week. She wasn't sure when she would do her usual Sunday-night planning for the week ahead; she had told the family that the four of them would decorate the tree that night, and she was amazed when no one tried to get out of it.

Perhaps she shouldn't have been. Everyone had been a little more considerate, a little kinder, since Tim and Peter's car accident the month before. They also had less time to bicker, she reflected, as Willa was juggling school with an ever increasing set of demands from their candymaking, and Tim was busy working for her on the weekdays and assisting Shep in the store on Saturdays. Jennie had always planned to buy her son a used car or a van. After the accident, the plan changed. She and Shep had forbidden him to use either of their cars except to help at work; if he wanted to drive anywhere for his own purposes, he would have to buy a car and pay all the related expenses. He had come up with the idea of working for the two of them to offset part of the cost.

The best part, in Jennie's view, was that Tim and Shep left together on Saturday mornings and came home together at the end of the day. There was no more fighting or storming out. Evidently, Tim had grasped the deep pain behind Shep's confession to Peter that night by the side of the road, and it had made an impression. He had developed empathy for his father, something Jennie had never imagined she would see from him. Beyond that, it appeared that Shep's handling of the situation had won him respect from his son.

It had taken some time, but the fallout from the accident had subsided. The boys had gotten a good scare from the police and knew they were lucky to have gotten off with warnings and fines. Peter's family had hospital bills to contend with, but Jennie suspected the church community had arrangements for medical emergencies. Mattie didn't seem inclined to discuss the accident in any way, so Jennie didn't ask. She had seen the pain in Mattie's eyes that night when she met them at the hospital. They sat together, waiting to find out how badly Peter was injured, and they hugged when his shoulder injury turned out to be one that would heal without surgery. He would be in a sling for a while but was expected to recover fully. Even then Mattie had kept her thoughts to herself. When Jennie tried to explain how mortified she was that Tim had been involved, Mattie stopped her at once, saying none of it was Tim's fault. She told Jennie not to think for a second that Tim was responsible or to blame for anything at all, and it was clear she meant it.

Since then Tim had made time to go to the farm and help Peter with his work. It was indeed difficult for Peter to do much with his shoulder restrained by a sling. Efraim Fisher and his family had extended their stay through December, and the decision had been made to hire an Amish man to work with Peter in the early spring. All of Peter's siblings would be getting additional jobs in the barn come next spring, as they were another year older and more capable of helping.

The tree trimming that evening went remarkably well. Jennie and Willa used colorful raffia and ribbon scraps to create braided strands that draped around the branches. Everyone was in a good mood, sipping hot apple cider, the kids even horsing around. As far as Jennie was concerned, that was enough of a Christmas gift.

The next night, she and Tim were dropping off a batch of candy at the Fisher house when Peter decided to tell his mother how he felt about having to take over the family farm. He was pouring hot chocolate into a mug just as they arrived and apparently decided now was the right moment to speak. Sipping at his drink, he came to stand by his mother, who was repairing a torn bedsheet.

"Yes?" Mattie looked up at him.

"We must talk. About the farm and me."

Jennie froze. She could tell from the tone of his voice that this was going to be the big talk that Shep had advised him to have with his mother. Why was he doing it with her and Tim present? Safety in numbers, perhaps, she thought, or moral support.

Mattie put down her sewing as if sensing the conversation would be serious.

"I know how important farming is. I know it is what we believe is good and right." Peter took a breath. "But I don't want to be a farmer."

Mattie only nodded to indicate that she had heard.

"The farm is everything to us," Peter went on in an anguished tone. "I wish I wanted to run it."

"I know you do not want to farm. And that you wish you did want to."

Peter stared at his mother. "You know?"

"You've never wanted to be a farmer. But you understand that it is what is important and it is our lives."

He could only look at her in amazement. Thinking back, Jennie realized that Mattie had always known Peter didn't want to farm. She recalled the day Mattie visited when Jennie was recovering from the flu. How they'd talked about Peter's responsibilities and Mattie had hinted at his unhappiness.

"So what do I do?" Peter was almost whispering.

"You go on doing what you must do for now. You have your sisters and brothers to care for. We have people to help you, and we will hire someone in the spring. If that does not work, we will look at the situation. We must keep the family farm, but we will figure out if you can consider something else to do at some other time."

He exhaled as if he had been holding his breath. "Thank you."

Nothing more was said on the subject.

Even though he wasn't released from his obligations, the understanding that his heart lay elsewhere seemed to be all he needed. In the days that followed, Jennie saw how removing the burden of his secret made him happier. He laughed more, and the tension she had noticed in his expression fell away.

For her part, Mattie told Jennie that many things might happen between now and the spring, and she had faith that all would go well. Jennie admired, as always, her friend's wisdom and calm.

On Thursday, the Davises sat down to a quiet Thanksgiving meal, Scout in his usual position beneath the table, hoping for one of them to drop some tasty morsel or take pity on him and slip him some scraps. After everyone had filled their plates and started eating, Jennie leaned over to him.

"I trust you're down there reviewing what you have to be thankful for," she said as he lifted his head, alert to the potential of getting something special to eat.

"I don't think dogs feel things like being thankful," Tim said.

"Why not?" asked Willa. "They must appreciate it if you give them water when they're thirsty. Stuff like that."

"Well, I know that I'm thankful," Jennie said. "For so many things. First, of course, you guys. I'm thankful Tim wasn't hurt in the accident."

He frowned, clearly hoping she wasn't going to discuss it any further.

"Then the way everything has been going," she went on. "We're all doing well in lots of ways. I am genuinely thankful."

"Hear, hear," Shep said, raising his glass of cranberry juice and seltzer.

She hadn't said aloud that one of the things she was most grateful for was the fact that she hadn't seen her husband take a drink since the night of the car crash. Whatever it was—seeing his son get into trouble because of drinking, or maybe having confessed his own secret shame of feeling like a failure—he seemed to redirect his course. He no longer acted so put upon. Instead, he appeared to be filled with new resolve. The beers were gone, replaced by juices and soda.

After the meal, she found herself alone in the kitchen with Shep. He finished loading the dishwasher as she sponged down the counters. Perhaps, she thought, now was a good time to ask him the question she had wanted to ask for a while.

"So," she started, trying to keep her tone casual, "are you storing your awards and stuff? You want them to go in the basement, or will you be putting them back up?"

"They can go in the basement, sure."

Frustrated by his brief response, she pushed for more. "I thought I'd get the boxes out of the corner of the room, if you're absolutely sure you don't want to hang them up again."

"You're right. Sorry, I should have put them away."

She stopped what she was doing and turned to look at him.

"Shep, this is the first time you've taken down that stuff and boxed up your trophies. I guess I'm a little surprised."

He shut the dishwasher door and pressed the button to start the cycle. "It was time, that's all."

"Were you feeling so bad about things?" she asked as gently as she could.

He looked puzzled. "Bad? No." Understanding dawned on his face. "Is that what you thought?"

"Well . . ."

"Not at all. I just realized that it was bragging, nothing more. For another thing, it was time to stop looking back. There's what you do today, and that's all that counts. All the todays add up to a life."

She looked at him in surprise.

"I learned it from watching the Fishers, you know. First Abraham, then Efraim. They never brag about their accomplishments, much less plaster them up on their walls. They don't talk about the good stuff they've done for other people, either. They have no interest in personal glory. They live their faith, they take action."

"Mattie is all about taking action as well."

"Yeah, that's what they do."

"They sure take a lot of action," Jennie said with a smile. "I can't believe what that woman does in a day."

"The men, too. And they all have their jobs. Everybody knows what they're supposed to do. They operate like the proverbial well-oiled machine."

"Or like a team."

"A team . . ."

She could see he was remembering the same thing she was: that the two of them used to consider themselves a team.

Taking a few steps forward, he put his arms around her. He slowly brought her closer and kissed her. Without releasing her, he pulled back slightly and put his mouth to her ear.

"I'm so sorry," he whispered. "For everything. My pride almost destroyed us all. Pride, self-pity. I don't know why you're still here with me."

"Because I love you," she whispered back. "I can't imagine loving anyone else." In saying the words, she knew it was true.

"You've done an amazing job." He leaned back and looked in her eyes. "Starting with the move here. This business you've built is an incredible accomplishment. I don't know how you did it. And you've held the kids together when they were about to spiral out of control. Thank you, Jennie."

"I owe you an apology as well. Or about a hundred apologies." She smiled. "Somewhere along the line, I forgot that we were supposed to have each other's backs. You were unhappy, and I got mad at you for being unhappy. You wouldn't let me do what I wanted to do. I guess I was mostly focused on that." She paused. "To be honest, watching you drink so much was scaring me to death. The thought of you becoming like my mother—"

His tone was contrite. "That was especially unfair to you, given what you went through with her."

"We stopped talking, Shep. Just flat-out stopped."

"My fault, and you know how I am, J—stubborn like a mule. Just ask my brother."

"Michael loves you. He does, underneath all that nonsense he has going on."

"I've always known that."

"He wants to help," Jennie said.

"He already has, hasn't he?"

"How do you mean?" He couldn't possibly know about Michael's generosity at Christmas.

"Not sure what the exact amount was, but you didn't buy the paint and kitchen linoleum with beads and trinkets, now, did you? The new rug for the living room? That money had to come from somewhere. I was too worried about you guys to insist you give it back, but too proud to admit that I knew about it. I've been the ultimate coward."

"It was awful, keeping that a secret. But you knew all along!"

"No more secrets, okay?"

"No more."

She leaned her head against his chest and closed her eyes with relief. They would be all right. The two of them would be a team once more.

Chapter 17

Just as Jennie was intent on figuring out how to repair the family, Shep was apparently thinking along the same lines. To her surprise, the next day he called her and the kids together and asked the three of them to brainstorm with him about how to improve the bike store.

"I've watched you build the candy business, and you're all ridiculously good at this stuff. So how about you turn your skills to bringing the store back to life? It's not doing too badly, but I know it could be doing so much better."

"What do you want us to do?" Tim asked.

"You've already helped me update some stuff since you started coming in," Shep said to him. "But now I want all of us to go over everything, top to bottom. What we sell, how we sell it, how it looks. I need fresh eyes. Just because I was too stupid to ask for your help before doesn't mean I can't fix that mistake. So what do you say? Will you help me?"

If anybody had told her that she'd hear her husband say those words, she'd have laughed, Jennie thought. Not only was he asking for help, he was asking their children for help. He had been watching their talents blossom over the past months and had come to appreciate them.

"How about if we all go to the store together?" Willa said. "It makes more sense to be there so we can see what we're talking about."

Shep gave her a quick salute. "First great idea."

"Brainstorming," Tim said. "All suggestions welcome, no matter how crazy, okay?"

"Absolutely," Shep said with a smile. "The crazier, the better."

"How do we decide what to act on? I have to believe some of these suggestions are going to cost money," Jennie put in.

Shep turned to her. "You and I can decide if and what we're willing to spend, okay?"

"Fine," she answered. "We'll assume the sky's the limit, then take it from there."

That Sunday, Shep and Tim went ahead to the store while Jennie and Willa finished their candymaking tasks. When Jennie pulled her car into a parking spot outside the store, an excited Scout jumped out to run ahead of them. Jennie entered and heard the jingle of the bell above the door. She saw at once that the space was a lot cleaner than she remembered it, and the area near the front door had been cleared.

"Anybody here?" she called out.

"In the back," Shep answered.

He and Tim came up front, Shep bending down to pet

Scout, who jumped up on him as if they hadn't seen each other in months.

"More space up here," Jennie observed.

"We want to put a counter up front, but we're waiting to go over everything with you guys. Let me show you."

Tim started to outline some of his suggestions. Jennie was astonished to see that he took genuine pleasure in laying out ideas for the store. Before she could say a word, Willa and he started tossing ideas back and forth.

"Dad should be selling lots of other stuff besides the bikes," Tim said. "I've got a whole bunch of websites and catalogs. Not just helmets, which he has already, but clothes, pumps, water bottles—everything you need or could want when you ride." He pointed to one wall. "Here's where we want to put gridwall to display it. This side would be for slatwall—where you display sneakers and great shoes for biking."

"Have you seen some of the fancy bikes around here?" Willa asked. "Dad should be selling the special seats, stuff like that. Do you offer customized paint jobs on the bikes, Dad?"

"No one's asked," he said in amusement at his daughter's businesslike tone. "But I could make that happen."

"I vote for a paint job for the whole place," Jennie put in. "You know I'm a big believer in a new coat of paint."

"Carpeting? Is that possible?" Willa again.

"Depends on how much we're willing to invest, folks," Shep said.

"New lighting would be pretty great, too." Tim made a rueful face, acknowledging how expensive that would be.

Shep grabbed a yellow pad and a pen. "Whoa, too many ideas. We need a list."

The children were just getting warmed up. Tim was in favor of building a website, and Willa wanted it to show that the store was concerned about the environment and how cycling promoted healthy living. "No car exhaust, healthier for your body—"

"Hold it," Shep said, writing furiously.

"An online newsletter," Tim chimed in, "featuring events in the store and activities you'll be promoting."

"Is it possible to have a mechanic—you or someone else—in back, and a salesperson up front?" Jennie asked. "People shouldn't have to work to find a person to help them."

"Let's hang some of the bikes on the wall. Or maybe a bunch going upward in a row, like they're riding up the wall." Willa was looking over Shep's shoulder at his notes. "We haven't even talked about the window displays yet."

Shep stopped writing and looked over at Jennie. He grinned. "I didn't realize we had so many geniuses in the family," he said.

"These kids earn their keep," she said, returning his grin.

"It's a good thing we like you," Willa said, "or we wouldn't share our genius with you."

Shep leaned over to kiss the top of her head. "Good thing," he echoed.

"Ewww, stop." She pushed him away.

"I kissed my child," he said to Jennie. "Perish the thought!"

"*Daa-aad.*" Willa's voice rose to a whine, but her smile made it clear she was pleased.

When they were done compiling all their suggestions, they sat down with Tim's computer and a stack of catalogs and determined what they would order now and what could wait. The night before, Shep and Jennie had agreed to allocate three thousand dollars from both their earnings toward getting the project under way. Willa started placing actual orders online, while the other three moved bicycles around in anticipation of the changes in the store's layout. Then, armed with paper towels and spray cleaner, the four of them did a thorough cleaning, making sure every inch of chrome on the bicycles shone and every surface they could reach was cleaned.

It was after seven when they locked up the store for the night, exhausted. Only Scout, who had spent much of the day napping in a corner, had any energy left when they got home, bounding over to his food bowl and giving Jennie a questioning look.

"As if you did anything today to deserve this," she told him as she opened the dog food. "Really, once a freeloader, always a freeloader."

The family ate a quick dinner of grilled cheese sandwiches, which they agreed were the best things they had ever tasted, after the long, hard day. Shep was already sleeping when Jennie crawled into bed at ten-thirty and set her alarm clock. She wondered how she was going to get up early to start the busy day of candymaking ahead. Settling in under the covers, she felt Shep roll toward her in bed and, still asleep, put his arm around her. She closed her eyes, appreciating the warmth of him next to her. This was how she would get up in the morning, knowing they were on the road to becoming a family again.

She was slow getting started the next day, and by midmorning, she decided she needed some fresh air. Scout saw her pick up his leash and ran to her, delighted to see that he would be getting an extra walk. The sky was gray and the day cold, with the feeling of impending snow. Scout trotted alongside her as she scanned the horizon, the fields dormant, the animals keeping warm in the barns. She decided she loved the forbidding weather as much as the spring sunshine; it revealed the majesty of the rolling landscape in a different way.

Passing by the Fisher house, she was surprised to hear Mattie calling her name. She veered off the road toward the kitchen entrance. Mattie held the door open for her.

"Aren't you supposed to be working at the booth now?" Jennie asked, glad to step into the warmth of the kitchen, fragrant with the smell of fresh-baked bread.

Without asking, Mattie poured a cup of coffee, putting in milk to make it the way she knew Jennie liked it. "A schedule mix-up, so there were two of us assigned to one shift. I am happy to stay home today, though. There is much to plan."

"Oh?"

Mattie smiled. "I have news today."

Jennie smiled back, bringing the cup to her lips. "Good news, it sounds like."

"Zeke and I are getting married."

"What?" Jennie was so surprised, she almost spilled the coffee. She set it down on the counter. "Zeke, Barbara's brother? The one who visited, who was at my barbecue?"

"That Zeke, yes."

"But when . . ." She had so many questions, she didn't know where to start.

"You are one of the first to know we are getting married."

Jennie hugged her. "I'm honored. And I'm so, so happy for you!"

"Thank you. It is very good."

"Very good? It's wonderful!" Jennie grinned. "How did this happen? When have you even seen each other?"

"I have known him for many years, of course. Remember, Barbara is his sister, and she is my sister-in-law. He has visited here a couple of times since Abraham is gone."

"When is the wedding?"

"It will be in January."

"That's so soon!" Jennie was taken aback.

"The church service is first, then the afternoon and night are here. There will be a lot of food but many people help to cook and serve it." She reached to take Jennie's hand. "You and your family will come?"

"Nothing could keep us away. This is the most exciting thing ever."

Mattie smiled. "No, but it is happy news."

"He seemed so nice that day I met him."

Mattie's eyes seemed to brighten as she thought about him. "He is a good man, very good."

Jennie was thrilled to see the light in her friend's eyes, a light that seemed to have been permanently dimmed when Abraham died.

"Does this mean he will move here, to the farm?"

Mattie nodded. "He will work with Peter. Zeke has always wanted a farm, so now he will have this one to work."

"I remember him saying he wanted to buy one."

"Yes, he almost did. It is fortunate that he didn't, because then we would have a problem, with two farms in different places. We decided he should come here to live."

Jennie could only imagine how thrilled Peter must be to know that his mother was marrying a man who would be happy to run the farm. She hugged her friend again. "May I tell Shep?"

"Yes. It is not a secret. But I wanted to tell you myself."

They talked for another few minutes before Mattie had to excuse herself to attend to dinner preparations. Jennie and Scout continued on their walk.

"Can you believe it?" she asked the dog as she pulled her coat collar more tightly around her neck. "And he seems so great, too. This is the best news in the world."

Scout barked at something across the road.

"You are so right," Jennie said. "She totally does deserve it. I have to say, she's one of my favorite people, even though she would reprimand me if I told her that. You know she won't allow anyone to single her out for praise."

The day was growing colder, and she decided it was time for them to turn back for home. As she let herself in the front door, she heard the phone ringing and dashed to pick it up.

"J, is that you?"

It was Michael. She smiled, delighted to talk to another of her favorite people. "How are you," she asked, struggling out of her coat while holding the receiver, "and how was your Thanksgiving?"

There was a brief silence on the other end. "Fine, thanks." His words were terse.

Uh-oh, she thought. That didn't sound good.

"Anyway," he went on quickly, "I wondered how you would feel about some uninvited guests popping in for Christmas."

"You guys want to come to us? That would be great." She was pleased to realize that she meant it. This year she and her family were doing so well; it would be a very different holiday.

"Not all of us guys, no. Just me and the kids. For a few days."

She hesitated, then decided it wasn't appropriate for her to ask questions. "Of course, Michael. We'd love it. Come whenever and stay however long you like."

"Great." He sounded relieved. "We'll fly in and rent a car. Would it be okay if we came on the twenty-third?"

"Sure. Would you like to stay over with us? We can do a little shifting around to make room."

"Could we? That would be terrific."

She had meant the offer but was shocked that he'd agreed to it rather than choosing a luxurious hotel. "That'll be a huge treat for us," she said.

"I have to run to a meeting now, but I'll call again with the timing when we get closer. Bye and thanks. Best to my brother and the kids, okay?"

He hung up.

The first thing she thought was how surprised Shep would be to hear that his brother was coming to stay with them and coming without his wife. Still, maybe she was making something out of nothing. Maybe Lydia had to be someplace. That didn't make sense, though; he always spent Christmas with Lydia and the children. If he could fly here for the holiday, then he could fly wherever she might be, too. Maybe it was the way he had responded to the question about Thanksgiving that was giving her a bad feeling. She hoped there wasn't trouble at home, and she couldn't help thinking about her niece and nephew, crossing her fingers that they wouldn't have to deal with bad news.

As she put down the telephone receiver, Scout came up to her and nuzzled his face against her leg. She scratched under his chin, lost in thought about the contrast in her two encounters this morning.

Chapter 18

With the help of a flashlight, Jennie walked through the chilly darkness to the mailbox, using the trip as an excuse to get a breath of fresh air. After spending so many hours working without a break, she needed a minute to clear her head. She reached into the box and extracted a pile of envelopes and circulars.

"Bills and more bills," she muttered, flipping through the stack. She pulled out a square envelope, addressed by hand and personally delivered by the writer, as evidenced by the lack of a stamp. "Wow—a piece of actual mail from a human being!"

The envelope contained a handmade Christmas card from the Fishers, an angel colored with markers and decorated with glitter. She was late in mailing out their holiday cards and decided she would talk to Willa about making their own instead of sending out the usual boring store-bought ones. The effort put into the Fishers' card was touching, and the sentiment clearly genuine. As usual, she thought, if she followed their guide, she couldn't go wrong.

She went into the dining room, which had been converted into a shipping station, with cartons, packing tape, and scissors arranged to speed the process of getting packages ready to go. Shep, Tim, and Willa were all there, working as fast as they could to pack the bags and tins of peanut brittle and lollipops into appropriate-sized brown boxes. It was fortunate, she and Shep had agreed, that the bicycle business slowed down for the season as her business picked up, because he was able to help fulfill the orders. As Christmas drew closer, the four of them worked frantically not to fall behind.

As if they had time to make cards, she thought. What had she been thinking? They could barely keep up with all they had to do as it was.

"Check out this lovely card from the Fishers," she said, holding it up. No one even glanced over. She went into the living room to prop it up on the mantel next to the few others they had received, then returned to the dining room to pitch in with the packing. "Shep, did you ever get out your customer holiday cards?"

"Yup. All done." He didn't look up from the carton he was taping shut.

"That's great. I'm sorry I forgot to ask before." She sat down at the open laptop to check if any new orders had come in over the past half hour.

"By the way," he went on, "I just got in a bunch of new bike accessories, so I hope somebody will help me get them on display at some point."

"No problem," Tim said.

Jennie looked over at her son. Even though he was working long hours for her and Shep, he'd been able to find time to spend with some new friends he had made at school. It had taken him almost a year and a half, but at last he was settling in with people he liked. That had seemed to be the final missing piece for him, and he was no longer at the mercy of his temper; he had let go of most of the anger he had been carrying around when they first moved here. On top of that, the more time he spent with his father, the better they got along. Tim had been willing to open the door to a new relationship with his father, and Shep had been only too glad to go through it.

Willa's voice interrupted her reverie. "If we get a big rush in the last twenty-four hours before deadline, we're going to be in trouble, Mom."

"I have an idea. Do you think we could hire Evie and her mother for that week, let's say the nineteenth to the morning of the twenty-fourth? I know it's short notice . . ."

Evie was Willa's friend from school, and Jennie had met the girl's mother several times when they were picking up or dropping off their daughters at each other's houses. The mother had mentioned to Jennie that she was looking for work.

"I'll ask."

"I like her mother," Jennie reflected aloud. "Maybe I could invite them over for dinner one night."

"Just make it after the holidays, okay?" Willa asked. "I'm ready to fall asleep with my head in my plate most nights."

"It'll be over soon," Shep reassured her. "Let's just be grateful we have such a problem—being too busy."

"If all goes well, in the spring you'll be just as busy at the shop," Jennie said. "It looks great. People are going to be really surprised by everything that's going on."

Although they hadn't followed up on some of the more expensive plans, all four of them had been involved in carrying out a lot of their brainstorming list for the store. The website was up, and Willa gave Tim information to add to it whenever she could find the time. She was also working on a green campaign to encourage biking. Tim had set up software so they could view the buying histories of their customers and inform them of new items that might be of interest, or point out what was old or perhaps missing in their gear. He liked combining his computer skills with business, and Jennie was amazed on several occasions to find him in his room reading industry newsletters about cycling. She wished she could help out more, but the three of them had handled the lion's share of it and seemed to be doing an excellent job without her. The store wasn't physically transformed yet, although they were working toward that goal, and the new sky-blue paint made it brighter and more inviting. They were cautiously hopeful about the upcoming spring season.

The next morning, she got up at five to make candy and deliver it to the Fishers for the market booth and packaging.

When she entered the kitchen, she saw Nan straightening Joshua's shirt as he recited a poem.

"Good morning," she said to Jennie. "My brother is practicing for the school Christmas program."

The little boy nodded. "I say the poem for all our parents and guests. Everyone comes to the school, and we do skits and read stories. I will recite this poem."

"It's a big event for the children," Nan added, smoothing down his hair.

"I can imagine," Jennie said. "It sounds lovely, Joshua."

"That's enough," he said to his sister, squirming away from her and running out of the room.

"Take your lunch," she called after him.

He raced back in, making a wide circle as he grabbed a lunchbox and thermos before running out again without stopping.

Nan smiled. "He was worried I might try to fix his clothes some more."

"You all take such good care of one another," Jennie observed as she put the shopping bags on the kitchen table.

Nan shrugged. "The little ones need help. That's all."

Jennie thought of her own children's incessant fighting, quelled now and hopefully for good. Suddenly, she recalled that she would have Michael's children in her home again soon, and she wondered if they would be any different. After a year spent among the Amish and their children, she didn't know if she would have the stomach to watch the two complain about every little thing. Her next thought was that their mother wouldn't be with them. She frowned, hoping that Lydia's absence didn't signify trouble; whether the children were spoiled or not, it would break her heart if anything serious had happened to their parents' marriage.

By the time the twenty-third arrived, Jennie was too exhausted to worry any further about the state of Michael's marriage. Got To Candy had promised its customers that all deliveries received by that date would be shipped in time for Christmas Day arrival, and it was a vow she realized she had been unprepared to keep. If things went as well next year, she would hire more people for the holiday season, but that was little comfort now as they struggled over the handmade labels and wrappings. She told Shep to warn his brother that they might get spaghetti for breakfast, lunch, and dinner, but there was all the peanut brittle the kids could eat.

When Michael and the children arrived late in the afternoon, Jennie glanced down at her old sweater, jeans, and sneakers and realized she hadn't even put on any makeup that day. It was lucky they had managed to hang the Christmas decorations around the house; no time to decorate herself, she thought.

Scout, as usual, got to their guests first, followed by Shep, who was welcoming everyone over the barking when she joined them. No fancy overcoat and blazer for Michael this year, she noticed. He wore a parka over jeans and a flannel shirt. Evan and Kimberly were a little taller, and Jennie fussed over how much more grown-up they looked, which both of

them liked. Beyond that, she could tell their demeanors were
more subdued, their expressions almost somber. Michael gave
Jennie a shopping bag with two store-wrapped gifts for Tim and
Willa, which told Jennie that Lydia hadn't picked them out;
she invariably did her own special gift wrapping.

Tim and Willa came out to greet their uncle, then ushered
their little cousins back into the dining room, planning to put
them to work taping boxes, at least until they got bored with it.
The adults went into the living room.

"Nice tree," Michael said, barely glancing at it.

"Willa and I used leftover paper to make the braids." Jennie
saw he wasn't listening and stopped. "Sit down, Michael, and
let me get you a soda or something."

"Great."

She and Shep exchanged glances, registering that Michael
was nervous, completely out of character for him. They
wouldn't ask any questions, she decided, but let him relax and
get to it all in his own good time.

They made small talk for a bit. Michael wanted to hear all
about their candy business and walked around the dining room,
examining the lollipops and tins of brittle. Dinner was pizza in
the living room, the only place with space to seat them all.

"Please excuse the takeout, Michael," Jennie said as she slid
the pieces onto paper plates. "As you can see, it's just too crazy
to cook. You probably thought I was kidding when I said you
wouldn't get any good food this trip."

He grinned. "Are you kidding? First of all, this is great.
What's better than relaxing with pizza? Second of all, I couldn't

be happier for you guys. You're building this business with no investment to speak of. It's fantastic."

"I have to get everything out of here by tomorrow so it can be delivered on Christmas Day. After that, we can all collapse," she said.

"No, then you have to get ready for Valentine's Day," Shep put in. "You guys said you were going to bring in something new."

Willa, seated next to him, gave an exaggerated groan and a wild-eyed look to her cousins. Evan and Kimberly laughed and began imitating her groan. "That's right," she encouraged, "let everybody know how put upon I am. Make 'em feel sorry for me."

The children grew louder and, following Tim's lead, got up to make piteous faces and fall to the floor. Jennie laughed, delighted to see Michael's children acting like kids instead of small adults. The cell phones, she realized, were nowhere in evidence. As Kimberly sat back down next to her, Jennie put an arm around her niece, whose pleased expression gratified her. After a dessert of ice cream with chocolate sauce, Jennie suggested the children take a break upstairs, saying she would be working later on, and if they were up to it, they could come back.

"You sure we can go?" Tim asked.

"Please, you need some time to relax. Besides," she said with a smile, "we're doing well with our schedule but not that well. We'll get tonight's stuff done if Dad and I give it an extra push later."

"You don't have to say it twice." He led the others upstairs.

"More coffee?" Shep asked his brother.

Michael shook his head. "I still have some. But I want to thank you two for letting me just be here without any explaining. That dinner was perfect, and the kids and I both needed it."

"You needed pizza? I hear they have excellent pizza in Chicago," Jennie said in a light tone.

He smiled. "No, we didn't need pizza. We needed *normal*." His expression grew serious again. "We haven't had any normal in some time."

"What's going on, Michael?" Shep asked in a gentle voice.

"I don't know where to start." He leaned back on the sofa and stretched out his legs. "It started with me, really. A couple of years back. I was getting tired of the way we were living. I did nothing but work, except when we took these extravagant vacations, where I still did nothing but work, only it was on my phone or laptop. Mind you, I drove myself to get to that point, where I was a big important guy who always had a phone glued to his ear and a million people clamoring for advice or decisions."

"You're a successful lawyer. That's got to come with the territory," Jennie said.

"It wasn't only that. I was making a lot of money, but I hated what we were doing with the money. The mindless spending— on clothes and gadgets and junk for the kids. Sometimes I felt like all our junk was going to rise up and suffocate me."

"I never realized you felt that way," Shep said.

"It was creeping up on me. And the kids were getting so spoiled. It must have been going on for a long time before I woke up enough to see it. It wasn't just that they expected someone else to pick up after them, do their bidding. That was bad enough. But they weren't *kind*. They didn't care about anything or anyone. Once I saw that, it became obvious." He took a sip of his cold coffee. "I was so embarrassed last Christmas by the way they behaved here, and that was nothing compared to other things I'd seen them do. Anyway, I tried to talk to Lydia about it. Got nowhere."

"She didn't agree with your assessment of things?"

"That's one way to put it. She was furious that I would dare question how, as she put it, she was raising the children. When I suggested that some of our values might be a little out of whack, she really hit the roof. She worked so hard to give me this beautiful life and so on."

"She did work hard at making things nice." Jennie recalled the meticulous attention to detail in Lydia's clothes, her makeup, whatever she did.

"When we were here last year, I realized what nonsense that all is. You guys have a family, not the trappings of a family, which was what I had."

"Boy, you really didn't understand what was—" Shep started.

"There was life happening here," Michael burst out. "In our house, there was no life. Just schedules and appointments. Tutors and choosing the right everything. It was one big competition to stay a step ahead of whoever Lydia decided was important."

Shep leaned forward. "Why are you talking in the past tense?"

Michael looked down. "She must have realized things were not going in the direction she wanted. She found somebody else."

"Ohhhh . . ." Jennie breathed.

"Not just anybody else. An Italian guy she met at some charity function. With way more money than I have and no problem showing it off."

"You're getting a divorce?" Jennie asked.

He nodded. "And she's moving to Italy. Without the children. She says she'll come back in a few months and take them on a vacation. *Vacation*, for goodness' sake!"

There was silence as Shep and Jennie took this in.

"Guess they'd be in the way," Michael said with bitterness. "Hard to believe she could pick up and leave them like that, but that's what she's doing. One day they were the most important things in her life, according to her, and the next, they were of just about no concern at all."

Jennie tried to hide the shock she was afraid showed on her face. "Do they know what's going on?"

"They know that we're splitting up and she's going to Italy with this man. I don't think they understand she's going away pretty much for good. That they'll be lucky if she drops in for a visit once in a while."

No one spoke.

Finally, Michael stood up. "I did quite a job picking a wife, didn't I?"

"Don't say that," Shep said. "You couldn't have foreseen all this."

"Yes, yes, I could have. The way she is—it was right in front of me, but I didn't want to see it." He looked at his brother. "You saw it. I must have realized that, and I didn't want to hear you say it."

"Be fair to yourself," Jennie protested. "You were married a long time, and that was an accomplishment."

"It was a long time because I was never there. Always working, traveling. I let everything important fall by the wayside. Like you guys."

"We've always been here," Jennie said. "And we know you cared a—"

"Come on, J, don't humor me," he said. "I haven't forgotten the way things used to be, how close we three were. That was all lost."

Shep came over to put a hand on his shoulder. "So what are you going to do now?"

"No idea. Now it's going to be about my kids, getting them through this shock. Then we'll have to figure out what kind of life the three of us will want to live. All I can tell you is that it's not going to be the one we were living."

"Tell us how we can help."

"Letting us come here for the holiday was a big one. I don't know what would have happened if the three of us had been alone at home. It would have been awful."

"We'll get through tomorrow, and then we'll spend all our time with the children." Jennie turned to Shep. "In fact, let's ask if Evie and her mom will take a double shift, so we can stop working about midday tomorrow."

"Good idea."

"No," Michael said, "I don't want you paying out extra money because of us. But hey, why can't we three help? I've been known to move pretty quickly when I have to. Maybe if we find something my kids can do, we can speed things along."

"Okay, then," Jennie agreed. "Welcome to the staff of Got To Candy."

She went upstairs to check on the children, her mind racing with what she could do to provide some comfort to her niece and nephew. Shep and Michael sat back down to talk some more. Out of so much sadness, she thought, at least there was this one good piece: The brothers had each other again.

Chapter 19

When Jennie heard the doorbell ring, she hoped with all her heart that it wasn't one of her deliveries being returned. It hadn't been easy, but with everyone—including Michael and his children—working at a furious pace, they had kept Got To Candy's guarantee.

She pushed her chair back from the table, gesturing for everyone else to stay put. Shep, Michael, and all the children were eating roast chicken, string beans, and baked potatoes, the best impromptu meal she could throw together after they got the last box out. She was fascinated to see that Evan and Kimberly ate without complaint, free of cell phones or other distractions.

At the moment, they were engaged in a discussion of the best desserts they had ever eaten, and they barely noticed her leave the room. She was still considering possible shipping errors as she went down the hall. Scout was already barking at the door, frantic to learn the identity of their visitor.

"Come on, Scout, please stop the racket!" The dog barked louder. "You know, sometimes—" she said in a threatening tone as she turned the doorknob.

A woman stood outside in the freezing darkness, several feet away from the door as if hesitant to get too close, bundled up in a long coat against the snowy night. The thick woolen scarf wrapped around her neck and lower portion of her face obscured almost everything but her eyes.

"Yes?" Jennie peered out in the dimness of the porch light.

"Jennie?" The woman took a small step forward and loosened the scarf to reveal more of her face.

Jennie stared at her. How many times over the years had she imagined this very thing? she asked herself. Early on, she had wished with all her heart that it would happen, that Hope would reappear out of the blue the same way she had disappeared. Later, though, she grew angry and hurt. When she pictured her sister coming back, she envisioned herself lashing out, wanting to punish her the way her absence had punished Jennie. It had taken so many years to harden her heart to her sister, getting to the point where she accepted—where she genuinely believed—that she would never see Hope again. The mixture of feelings had been buried along with her memories, and for the most part, she had been successful at keeping them buried.

Yet here Hope was, and all those feelings came rushing back.

"Hope," Jennie whispered.

The other woman nodded. "Yes. It's me."

Her face was drawn, and the wrinkles etched in it made her look older than Jennie knew she was. Whatever she had been doing with her life, it must not have been easy.

"Why?" Jennie was stumbling over the words. "Why are you here?"

As if she hadn't heard the question, Hope dropped her gaze to Scout, sitting at attention next to Jennie. He seemed to understand that now was not the time for him to create any further commotion. "Nice dog." Hope knelt and extended her hand for him to sniff. He got up to move toward her.

Jennie grabbed him by the collar. "Sit!" she commanded, and he obeyed at once. "I asked why you're here. And why now?"

Hope straightened up. "I guess I didn't expect you to be glad to see me, but I wasn't expecting quite this level—"

"Of what?" Jennie snapped. "Anger? No, make that fury. You expected the person you abandoned to welcome you with open arms?"

The wind was picking up.

"Do you think I might come in?" Hope asked. "It's pretty windy. Believe it or not, I've been standing out here for a long time, trying to get up the courage to ring the bell."

"With good reason." Jennie herself was freezing just standing in the doorway, and she could guess that Hope must be extremely cold by this point. Exasperated, she stepped back to make room for her sister to enter. Hope stepped over the threshold but made no effort to go any farther. As she un-wrapped the scarf fully, Jennie saw that her sister's brown hair, once thick and shining like her own, was dull and prematurely shot through with gray.

"Jen, who is it?" Shep called out from the dining room.

"That's my husband," she informed Hope.

"I know."

"You *know*?" Jennie held up a finger as she raised her voice to answer him. "It's okay, Shep, I got it." She turned back to her sister. "How do you know?"

"I've kept track of you all these years. You must realize that. Remember, I sent mail to you."

"Oh, now we're getting to it. The money! Is that what you're here about? You want it back, right?"

Hope shook her head. "Nope. Not at all. I just came to see you."

Jennie saw the old scar on Hope's jaw, an inch-long indenta-tion that was faded but visible, where she had cut herself when she fell out of a tree they were climbing. That must have been thirty years ago. The scar was as familiar to Jennie as if it had been on her own face. In an instant, she was back there, watch-ing the blood gush from the gash, a terrified five-year-old crying as she ran to get help.

Her emotions in turmoil, Jennie felt immobilized. She didn't know how she was supposed to treat her sister. Worse, she didn't know how she was supposed to feel about her. She was angry, but she was also aware that *her sister had come back*. On her own, the way Jennie always dreamed she would.

"Are Tim and Willa here, too?" Hope asked.

"You know their names?"

"Of course. Computers, you know . . ."

"Well, you're quite the devoted aunt."

Hope sighed. "I deserve that."

"So you also know when Mom died? That's when the money stopped coming."

A nod.

"Jennie, is everything all right?" Shep's voice was concerned. "We're waiting to hear if you would pick the cheesecake from that place just outside Lawrence over the pecan pie we had on our tenth anniversary in Boston. Remember that?"

"Be right there," she called back.

"It was wrong for me to come tonight. Maybe I should come back another time," Hope said. "I'm staying at a motel nearby, so I could wait until after you celebrate Christmas tomorrow. The next day, maybe."

"You'd wait around?"

Hope gave a wan smile. "This is what's important, so I'll wait as long as it takes."

"I don't get it!" Jennie exploded. "Why have you materialized on my doorstep?"

Her sister looked directly into her eyes. "I've wanted to see you for years. But I didn't think you'd ever forgive me. I was living in Phoenix, and I sold my house. The day I left, I got to thinking it was time to see you, not because I wanted to—which I did—but because I needed to make it right. Or try to."

"So you decided to come here all the way from Arizona on a whim."

"It wasn't a whim at all. But I've always lived like that. From the day I left home, I never wanted to get stuck in one place, like I felt stuck in our house. Makes me feel as if I'm suffocating. Anyway, the point is, I've never stopped feeling bad about leaving you behind. Leaving you alone with her."

"Then why did you?" Jennie wanted to shake Hope. "I was too young to be in charge like that. I had to take care of her, me, the house, everything. I was a kid!"

"I couldn't stay there. And I knew she wouldn't hurt you."

"No, *you* hurt me! Everything she did hurt me. You abandoned me—but she did, too. Just in a different way."

Hope's voice got quiet. "I meant hurt you physically. Like she did to me."

Jennie stared at her. "What are you saying?" It came out as a whisper.

"She used to hit me when she got drunk, a lot and pretty hard. With one of Dad's belts. She blamed me for him leaving us. Soon as I could, I got out. You were the only one she really loved, and I was dead certain she would never do that to you."

"She never did." Jennie was thinking back, horrified at the knowledge of what must have been going on in the house. "But I didn't know. How could that be happening and I didn't know?"

"She never did it when you were awake. At least some part of her brain realized it was wrong and knew enough to hide it from you."

Jennie was at a loss for words.

"So I left, and I never stopped leaving. Every place and everyone. I wished all the time that I had taken you with me, but I couldn't have had you on the road with me. Your life would have been much worse." Hope sighed. "And I knew you'd get through school if you stayed. The day you got married was one of the happiest of my life. Mom was gone and you had a real chance at having a normal life." She glanced around. "Which, it seems, you do."

Jennie was dumbfounded. "You tracked me all these years."

"I never stopped loving you, Jen. You're my baby sister. But I had to leave. If she didn't kill me, I was afraid I would kill her. But I never would have let anyone harm you."

"Where did you get all that money you sent?"

Hope shrugged. "Waitressing, mostly. I saw lots of places, had a lot of adventures. Mostly good, some not so good. I worked all over. Racetracks, funeral homes, you name it."

"Those don't sound like places that paid enough for you to send me money all the time."

"I didn't spend much. You needed money, and I got my freedom. It seemed like a fair deal."

Jennie was trying to absorb what she was hearing. It was too much to take in, she realized. Everything she'd believed about her childhood would have to be reexamined. "You've been moving around your whole life?"

Hope grimaced. "Most of it, but not the whole time. There was one person I didn't leave. My husband, Tom. We got married fifteen years ago. We were living in Michigan. I must have been there about seven years, which was a record for me. We had a son." She paused. "My husband and he were killed when he was two. Tom was pushing him in the stroller, crossing the street. Hit-and-run driver. Truck."

Jennie gasped.

"I left Michigan right after that."

Before Jennie could say anything, Shep appeared in the hallway, napkin in hand. "Honey, what's going on?" He stopped as he saw they had a guest. "Oh, excuse me, I didn't realize."

Jennie took a deep breath. "Shep, I want you to meet someone."

He came forward, smiling, extending a hand in preparation to shake.

"This is my sister, Hope."

The smile disappeared, and his hand fell to his side. "You're Hope." Said in a flat voice, it wasn't a question.

"Yes. Jennie didn't know I was coming here tonight, but here I am."

"Here you are, indeed." Anger on his wife's behalf was evident in his tone. He had met Jennie after Hope left town, but he knew the entire story and all the pain her disappearance had caused Jennie.

Hope didn't try to deflect his anger, only stood there returning his gaze.

Jennie couldn't handle the silence any longer. "This is all a little much to resolve in the hallway tonight." She turned to

Hope. "I guess it's going to happen one way or another, so you might as well come meet everybody else."

"This is what you want, Jen?" Shep sounded skeptical.

She looked from one to the other. "I don't have any idea what I want. But it's Christmas Eve, so we're going to sit down at the table and finish eating. For now, that's all I can manage."

Chapter 20

When Jennie got out of bed the next morning, she realized that snow must have been falling throughout the night. From her bedroom window, she saw a lush and silent landscape of white. A perfect setting for Christmas, she thought, pulling her robe's sash more tightly around her.

Glancing at the clock, she saw that it was seven-fifteen. Shep was still asleep as she tiptoed out of the room. A quick check revealed that everyone else in the house was sleeping as well. Tim had vacated his room for his uncle Michael and Evan. Willa was on a sleeping bag on the floor of her room, having given her bed to Kimberly for the night. Downstairs, Jennie peeked into the living room to find her son gently snoring on the couch with a quilt thrown over him. It was incredible that no one else was up yet on Christmas morning, she mused as she went into the chilly kitchen. Scout came padding into the room.

"It's just you and me, my friend," she murmured as she filled the carafe with water and measured out enough coffee for a full pot. It didn't take long for the aroma to fill the air.

The late sleepers shouldn't surprise her, she thought, recalling what time they'd all gone to bed. To say it had been a strange Christmas Eve didn't come close to describing it. Her brother-in-law had heard the story of Jennie's missing sister long ago, but his children had no idea their aunt had this mysterious sibling. Willa and Tim knew only the broadest outlines of what had happened; Jennie had never wanted to paint a negative picture of Hope for them. All she had told them was that she'd grown up with a sister who'd moved away and lost touch. Athough for different reasons, everyone's face wore an expression of shock when she introduced Hope.

Jennie refilled Scout's water bowl, thinking that, oddly, the dog had taken an immediate liking to her sister, planting himself beside her feet for most of the night. Hope's nervousness was revealed in the way she continually petted him and scratched behind his ears, the dog acting as friendly as she had probably hoped the other humans would be. Well, she had been out of luck there, Jennie thought as she set out the bowl and took a cup of coffee to the table. Michael and Shep had been minimally polite. Kimberly and Evan had, quite logically, lost interest in the adults within a few minutes and disappeared upstairs. Even Tim and Willa, fascinated at first, found the awkwardness among the adults to be tedious and followed their little cousins soon after.

The conversation had been awkward. Jennie was fighting off

the assault of conflicting feelings, not wanting to say too much or too little. Every time she started to think that she could patch things up with her sister somehow, that they could repair the damage of the past years, her good intentions were replaced by a cold sense of rage. Hope could come up with all the justifications she wanted, but it wouldn't change the fact that she had run away and left Jennie to fend for herself.

Her husband and brother-in-law made small talk about some of the places Hope had lived, but that went only so far. None of them was willing to talk about what was actually on their mind. At around eleven, Hope got up, insisting it was time she get back to the motel. It was a relief to Jennie to know the house was already full; she couldn't have extended an invitation to Hope to stay over even if she had wanted to. Which she did not.

There hadn't been an opportunity to discuss any of it with her husband or Michael after Hope had driven away. The children came trooping downstairs, wanting to make popcorn. After that, they started a game of Pictionary. Jennie was happily shocked to see her teenagers engaging unself-consciously with their little cousins, and she was able to put her thoughts aside as she got caught up in their laughing and shouting. Before anyone realized, it was two in the morning, and it took another half hour to get everyone settled into a bed or sleeping bag. When Jennie got into bed at last, she could almost believe she had imagined Hope's visit altogether. It was the best and the worst Christmas Eve of all, she reflected, sliding closer to Shep. Her sister had stirred up some of the most painful memories of Jennie's life. Yet she had also seen her children sharing a holiday with family, in the way the word "family" was meant to be used.

Her thoughts were disturbed by the sound of Kimberly and Evan coming down the stairs, talking in loud, excited whispers. She got up and sneaked over to stand by the kitchen doorway where they couldn't see her. The two children paused at the bottom of the steps. "Can we open our presents if no one else is here?" Kimberly whispered in an anxious voice.

"Sure," her brother said, all confidence.

"But Daddy won't—"

Jennie took a quick sideways step into the doorway and said in a booming voice, "Somebody here looking for Santa?"

The children jumped with fright.

"Aunt *Jennie*," Evan shouted, thrilled to be so scared.

The two of them ran over to her, shrieking as they lightly pummeled her in pretend anger.

"Okay," she said, "if that hasn't woken everybody up yet, you might as well get them up for present time."

They raced off, whooping. Wow, she thought, they were going to have a real Christmas morning. Humming, she decided to make pancakes along with the planned eggs and bacon.

Dressed in pajamas, the others assembled around the Christmas tree to open gifts. Everyone looked exhausted. Jennie served coffee to the two men, who were grateful to take the steaming mugs from her. Michael's children were by far the most energetic of the group, so they went first, pouncing on the boxes Jennie had wrapped for them. She had chosen a painting kit for Kimberly, with an assortment of oil paints, brushes, and cleaners. Evan received a set of artist's drawing tools: charcoal and colored pencils, erasers and a sharpener in a suede pouch. Jennie hoped they would like the low-tech gifts; something in her had rebelled against buying the two more gadgets.

"This is very cool," Evan said, sorting through his kit. He opened the accompanying gift, a flat package that turned out to be a sketch pad. "Neat!"

"Thanks," Kimberly added, unwrapping two blank canvases to go with her paints. "I can't wait to do this." She looked around anxiously. "Will somebody show me how?"

"Of course," Jennie said. "Absolutely."

It was hard to believe they were the same children who had been there the year before. Given some time to relax, and removed from all their displays of wealth, they were the loving children she remembered. If they hadn't yet grasped the truth of the situation at home, at least she knew they had a good foundation to support them in the painful times that lay ahead. With a pang for what they would soon have to face, she reached out to pull Kimberly to her for a hug.

The rest of the gift giving went by in a flash. Willa had requested a new backpack, and Tim wanted a pocketknife with lots of attachments, so they were both unsurprised but happy. Michael had brought the family a large wooden salad bowl with matching servers, along with an assortment of movies on DVD for the kids. Jennie was impressed that he'd made the time to pick out gifts, given his busy schedule and personal problems. After the wrapping was cleared away, he turned to his own children.

"Guys," he announced, "for your gifts this year, we're going to go to Uncle Shep's store and get you both new bikes."

"Yeah!" Evan held up a hand to his sister for a high five.

"Evan's outgrown his, and Kimberly is too small for his old one," Michael explained to Shep. "Not that she would ride a boy's bike. So it's time, and this is the place to get them." He turned to Jennie. "I also want to place an order with you, if I may. Can you ship some peanut brittle every month to us in Chicago? I'd pay you for a year in advance."

Jennie considered it. "I don't see why not."

"Great idea," Shep put in. "The Got To Have My Monthly Candy Division."

She smiled at him. "I like that."

There was the sound of a horse whinnying outside.

"Horse and buggy," Shep informed his brother. "Some of our Amish neighbors. Let's see if it's the Fishers."

Everyone went outside, where the sun had broken through the clouds. They saw two horses pulling buggies up the street. Through the windshield of the one in front, Mattie waved. Jennie realized that the man next to her, holding the reins, was Zeke. Peter was driving the second buggy.

"I wasn't expecting them today, but this is lovely." Hurrying to yank on her snow boots beside the door, Jennie got down the steps just as they were turning in to the driveway. All the younger Fisher children spilled out of the two buggies. They were dressed for the winter weather, the boys in wide-brimmed black hats and jackets, the girls in small dark jackets and bonnets.

"Merry Christmas to you," Mattie said, coming to greet Jennie with a hug. She wore a black bonnet and her heavy black shawl.

"And to you. What brings you here today? I thought you would be at worship."

Mattie shook her head. "No, that would only be if it was a regular Sunday for worship. We don't go to a special service because it is Christmas." She gestured toward the children. "We are home today, but we have some food to take near here."

Jennie gave her a questioning look. "What do you mean?"

"It is for two families. One of them has a very sick father, so the mother had no time to cook today. The other cannot afford it."

"Oh, Mattie, I didn't realize . . . You made Christmas dinner for other families."

"Yes. They need it."

Jennie smiled. "With all you have to do, you still managed that."

"Please do not think it was trouble for me. It was not. On this day in particular, it made me very happy to do it."

"I hope we can talk for a few minutes before you have to go. Please." Jennie gestured. "See, all the children are already playing together. So you can't go yet."

An informal snowball fight had started, which intensified when Shep, Michael, and Zeke got involved.

Mattie laughed. "Shall we walk?"

Jennie ran back to grab a jacket, and they set off together.

"You'll have your Christmas dinner later?" Jennie asked, squinting in the bright sunshine.

"Tomorrow." She saw Jennie's look of surprise. "We celebrate Christmas for two days. Today is more quiet. We will read Scripture, and later, the children will help me bake special cookies. Tomorrow is a day for visiting and a very big dinner."

"I didn't know."

"Also, tomorrow is Efraim and Barbara's last day. They are going. So are Red and his family. It will be a nice good-bye this way."

Jennie let out a wistful "Oh."

"Soon Zeke and I will be married, and we will run the farm."

"I'm so thrilled for you."

The Fishers would be a big, happy family again. The thought reminded Jennie of her sister, whom she had managed to drive from her thoughts all morning. When Hope left the previous night, she had asked Jennie to consider whether they should get together today. Jennie didn't know if she could face it all again.

"Mattie," she said, shoving her hands into her coat pockets. "I'd like to ask your advice about something."

"If I have something useful to say, I will be glad to say it."

"It's about my sister."

"I didn't remember you had a sister."

"No, you wouldn't. I never mentioned her to you."

Jennie went back to the beginning, back to the days when

her father lived with them, before her mother started drinking. Although her expression never changed, Mattie listened closely the entire time.

"I prayed she would come back, and now she has. But I'm so mad at her for what she did. She hurt me so much. I don't know if I can forgive her."

They walked along in silence for a few minutes, the only sound the snow crunching under their feet. At last Mattie spoke.

"It is hard for me to imagine this situation. Our families and our ways are so different. We are people just like you, and we have our problems. But we have rules and our church to advise us. To name one thing, no child would be running a house, like you did, without help.

"But it sounds like your sister suffered very much. When she was at home and later. She must have been so lonely. Even though she went away, she brought you along in her thoughts and prayers. She worked to make sure you would have enough to take care of yourself and your mother." She stopped and looked at Jennie. "The one thing I do understand is forgiveness. We believe in forgiveness. Your sister is asking you for this, yes?"

"Yes." Jennie's tone was grim. "But I'm not sure I can give it to her."

"Do you want to?"

Jennie turned away and gazed out over the beautiful landscape. At that moment, it felt to her like the most peaceful place on earth. The image of Shep and Michael came into her mind. Shep had never actually been angry with his brother, but she recalled the sorrow he had hidden over the years as the two drifted apart. It was obvious that his spirit was much lighter now that Michael was here and the gap between them was closing. She could tell it would be a new situation going forward, and they would have the good fortune to share their lives once again.

She considered what would happen if she sent Hope away without forgiving her, without letting her sister back into her life. It was more than likely that Hope would never return to ask again. She would slip through Jennie's fingers forever. The anger Jennie felt toward Hope was old, she reflected, so old it was fossilized, a rigid construct that served neither her nor anyone else. There was no joy in holding on to it. If she didn't do anything to change the situation, that anger would be with her forever. Along with the sadness of never knowing what might have developed between them.

Her voice was unsteady. "I believe I do want to forgive." Nodding with resolve, she repeated more firmly, "Yes, I believe I do."

"Well, then. You have your answer." Mattie smiled. "We should get back so we can give you a present. That is why we came over."

They turned around, and as they approached the house, Sarah came toward them holding a large bundle wrapped in tissue paper.

"Shep," Jennie called to him. "Mattie wants to give us something."

He was talking to Michael and Zeke, and the three men came to join them. The children clustered around to see what was going on.

"Oh, my," Jennie breathed as she pulled the tissue paper away to reveal a quilt, white with a repeating red geometric pattern.

"It's called Grandmother's Choice," Sarah explained.

Jennie unfolded it partially so it wouldn't touch the ground and held it up. "It's beyond beautiful," she breathed. "Look at the stitching . . ."

Willa stepped closer to peer at the pattern as she ran a hand along the surface. "I love this."

"You made it for us?" Shep looked amazed.

Mattie nodded. "Sarah and Barbara worked on it. Ellen, too."

Jennie had little doubt that Mattie had done most of the work herself yet would never mention it; she would consider that boastful. Barbara and Ellen weren't there, but Jennie's eyes found Sarah.

"Thank you so much," she said. "But oh, the hours of hard work, your time . . ."

"You have become special friends to our family," Mattie said. "It makes us happy to give you something that is special to us."

Jennie smiled. "We'll treasure it forever."

"Now we must go."

Mattie walked toward the horses, tied up at the mailbox, and her family followed, a few of the youngest running from their games in the snow to catch up. Zeke shook hands with Shep and Michael and said good-bye to Jennie.

At the last minute, Mattie seemed to think of something and walked back to Jennie. "Would you come to us for dinner tomorrow?" she asked. "You have your family visiting"—she nodded to Michael—"and it would be very nice if we could all sit down together. Also, you can see Efraim and Barbara and their family before they go."

"We're so many—it would be another seven people."

"That makes it even better."

Jennie laughed. "You have an answer for everything."

"Then it is settled. Come at twelve o'clock." She turned to go back to the buggy.

"They don't take no for an answer," Shep said with a grin.

Jennie smiled. "Never."

As the horses trotted away, the children called good-bye to Willa and Tim and their cousins from inside the buggies.

"That's quite a sight," Michael said to Jennie, who was clutching the quilt to her. "Looks like fun to ride in those."

"Everything they do is quite a sight," she said, staring after them. "Their simple lives are far richer than the lives of so many people. It's full of a special beauty, with its own rhythms. They know what they're about, and it gives them peace in their hearts."

She looked up at Shep and her brother-in-law. "Now, if you'll excuse me, I have to go call my sister."

Chapter 21

Kimberly and Evan were outside building a snowman when they saw the horse pulling an open sleigh, with Peter sitting in front holding the reins. He gave the slightest tug, and the horse stopped in front of the house.

"Thought you might like a ride," he called out. "Jump in."

"Seriously?" Evan asked. "We're waiting for everybody to drive over, but this would be awesome."

"We have to ask Dad," Kimberly reminded him.

"Ask me what?" Michael emerged from the house, pulling on his gloves.

"Can we please please *please* go? It's a real live sleigh!" Kimberly ran over and jumped up and down in front of their father as she begged.

"Look how cool it is, Dad," Evan said.

Peter called to Michael, "I'll just run them to the house, if it's okay."

"Sounds good to me. Thanks."

Tim must have heard Peter's voice, because he hurried out of the house as well, his jacket only halfway on. "I'm going with you guys."

Willa was right behind him. "Me, too."

"Is there enough room?" Michael asked.

"We have laps," Willa assured him as she ran by.

The four of them piled in, and Michael could hear his children's excited voices as Peter turned the sleigh around to go back to his house.

"What's up?" Shep was coming outside with Jennie.

"The kids went on ahead."

"Oh, a sleigh ride!" Jennie said, spotting them down the road. "I'll bet they're loving that."

Michael turned to them. "I can't thank you guys enough for this visit. The kids are having the greatest time."

Shep made a face of exaggerated apology. "It's no Aspen ski chalet . . ."

His brother laughed. Jennie was delighted to see that they were close enough to tease each other, the way they'd done in the old days.

"But listen," Michael said, his voice serious. "This has been the best thing we ever could have done this vacation. And it's been like a balm for me, too."

"We can assure you, the pleasure has been all ours," Shep said.

"Getting to know the kids again has been the biggest treat," Jennie added.

Michael kicked at the snow on the ground. "They've been banking good memories here. And I'm afraid they're really going to need them when we get home."

Jennie put a hand on his arm. "We'll be right here for them. And for you. Always."

They were interrupted by Hope's arrival. She lowered her car window as she pulled into the driveway. "Sorry I'm so late," she called out. "Shopping delayed me." She got out of the car and yanked open the back door. "Okay, ready to go," she said, reaching in for several bags.

"No rush. We just got ready ourselves," Jennie said.

Hope, too, must have felt their evening together had gone badly, because she was pleased but clearly surprised when Jennie called to ask if she would join them at the Fishers' today.

"I think we have to try again," Jennie said on the phone. "This could take us some time to get it right. But I want to try."

"That's the reason I'm here," Hope answered.

Now Jennie came forward to give her a hug. Her sister set several shopping bags of gifts on the ground and put her arms around Jennie in return. They stood that way for a long moment, years of things unsaid passing between them.

"Okay," Jennie finally said, taking a deep breath as she pulled away. "Let's go in my car." She turned toward the house and called, "Come on, Scout, you don't want to miss this afternoon, do you?"

The dog came bounding out. Jennie opened the car door, and he leaped in without breaking stride.

They arrived at the Fishers' house to find some of Mattie's

and Ellen's children coming toward the house, pulling sleds. Red-faced from the cold and the exertion of playing outside, they shouted excited hellos to the new guests. Hope whispered to Jennie that she saw candles in the windows but no other outside decorations to indicate the holiday.

Jennie nodded. "They don't have that. Some cards they made, maybe, some simple gifts. A big meal together. But it's about their faith. No Santa Claus, no tree."

"None of the commercial parts." Hope's tone was admiring.

"Never. They focus on what Christmas is really about."

As soon as they stepped into the house, they could smell the enticing cooking aromas. Mattie, Barbara, and Ellen were all moving around the kitchen, arranging platters, stirring steaming pots. A second table had been brought in to accommodate the guests. Jennie pointed out to Hope the handmade angels and stars displayed around the room, the only decorations aside from some greenery draped along the fireplace's mantel.

Mattie and Ellen left the stove to greet them, offering a special welcome to Hope. Jennie had asked permission to bring her, and the reply had been simple but instant agreement. "That will be very nice," was all Mattie said. As always, Jennie admired her friend's combination of directness and discretion.

The Davises had spent part of the morning wrapping gifts for the Fishers: a large book of photographs of horses, a reference book on bird-watching, board games, art supplies, and some accessories for the girls' dollhouse. For Sarah, the eldest, they brought a china serving bowl to go in her collection of fine dishes for her future home, a custom of Amish girls. Jennie understood she could bring only the practical for Mattie, nothing that suggested vanity or unnecessary adornment. The truth was, no gift she could imagine would be enough to thank the woman who had done so much for her. Still, she wanted to be respectful of the Amish traditions, so she chose a journal and two cranberry-scented candles. For the children, Hope had brought dried fruit and chocolate-covered pretzels as well as a large assortment of stickers with elaborate drawings of flowers and animals for the younger children. Mattie graciously accepted Hope's gift of two pies; Jennie didn't have the heart to tell her sister that they would undoubtedly be lost amid the sea of desserts certain to be in store.

"Where's Zeke?" Shep asked.

"He went back home early this morning."

"I'm sorry to hear that. We were in the middle of a conversation about planting a vegetable garden."

"Are you interested?" Jennie asked.

"Tim and I thought we might give it a shot in the spring."

"You should ask Mattie about that. She grows the fantastic vegetables here."

"Would you give me some advice?" Shep turned to her.

"Of course."

"That's great. But I'm still sorry I didn't get to see Zeke."

Mattie smiled. "He is with his family now. He will be back soon. To stay."

"With his new family," Jennie couldn't help adding. Not only was Mattie going to be married, but it seemed as if Shep might make a new friend. Jennie couldn't keep the smile off her face.

She was standing with Shep as the Fisher children scattered to put away their gifts. Peter approached them, carrying a brown paper shopping bag.

"I wasn't quite ready yesterday, and I'm not much of a wrapper," he said, a faint blush of embarrassment spreading across his cheeks. "But I made this for you. For your family."

He handed it to Shep, who opened the bag and extracted an intricately carved wooden birdhouse. "This is a beautiful piece of work," he said, turning it to admire the handicraft from every angle.

"You know we like birds, and I thought you might like to have them come to your yard, too." He looked down. "I wanted to say thank you for . . . well, for everything."

Shep put a hand on his shoulder just long enough to let it communicate their gratitude for his words. Jennie felt tears spring to her eyes. Not wanting to embarrass the boy any further, she kept silent.

"It is time," Barbara announced to no one in particular from the stove. "Dinner is ready."

Little by little, everyone reassembled in the kitchen and found their seats, men on one side of the table, women on the opposite. The long table was already set with freshly baked rolls and butter, pickles, and salad. After they said a silent prayer, the women and older girls got up to begin serving. Jennie and Willa assisted in setting out enormous platters of roasted

chicken, ham, mashed potatoes, noodles, and a variety of vegetables. Set aside on one corner of the counter for dessert, Jennie caught sight of two pecan pies, coffee cake and another pie
she couldn't identify, butterscotch and chocolate puddings,
multiple types of home-baked cookies and a chocolate cake.
They'll have to roll me out of here, she thought, but she didn't
care. Today was a day to celebrate and not worry about anything at all.

She took her seat again and looked around at everyone bus-
ily engaged in eating and conversation. Tim sat comfortably
next to his father, passing him a roll and laughing at something
he'd said. Willa was next to Nan and Sarah, looking so grown
up, Jennie thought as she recalled their first awkward meal at
the Fishers' house—it seemed so long ago—when her daughter
had been too shy and uncomfortable to speak to anyone. Willa
had truly come into her own, she mused, perhaps more than
any of them. Jennie allowed herself to bask in the joy it gave
her to work on the candy business with her child. That had
been another gift, completely unexpected. She took pride in
having started that business, although Willa probably deserved
equal credit for her inventiveness. Any way you looked at it,
the bonds that had been created between her and Willa were
worth far more than any business success.

Michael was on Shep's other side, leaning across the table to
pour milk for Kimberly. Despite the sadness she knew he was
feeling over the loss of his marriage, the lines of stress on his
face had eased in just the short time he had been with them.

Whatever difficulties awaited him, she had to believe he was on the right track in reclaiming his true nature, going back to the genuine person he was.

Next to her was Hope, the biggest surprise among the many surprises Jennie had experienced over the past year. She didn't believe it would be easy, but she knew that they were on the road to forming a new relationship. They would have to feel their way along, examining old wounds and questions, exposing to the open air everything that had been locked away for so long. It wasn't just Jennie's wounds; Hope had her own, and they would deal with all of them. Together.

Most wonderful and perhaps most miraculous was the transition in her marriage. She and Shep had come so close to the edge, she realized, it was frightening to consider what might have happened. Instead, they had rediscovered themselves and each other. The resentment that had smoldered beneath the surface had evaporated, which enabled them to see and feel clearly once again. There wasn't a drop of beer or alcohol in their house, and he started every day eager to get to his shop and see what new approach he could take toward making it grow. The enjoyment he was getting out of his work had transformed it from another experience to be endured to an opportunity to create his own business, one that he actually enjoyed.

Mattie was sitting at the opposite end of the table from Jennie but just then happened to catch her eye. Ah, Jennie thought, what would have happened without Mattie and this family? It was the Fishers who had shown her how to persevere. They moved forward no matter what the hardship or sorrow, without complaint, and always with humility. They looked for the best in one another, and they forgave with open hearts. Shep and their children had learned the lesson as well, she reflected, and from that had come so many good things. This one Amish family, with their hard work and simple joys, had taught them some very complicated lessons.

She smiled at Mattie, who smiled back but was distracted by Barbara asking her a question. She answered as she served another piece of chicken to one of the children. Jennie shook her head. As always, Mattie was the rock-solid heart of the household. Jennie thought of the quilt they had received yesterday. When she'd said they would treasure it, she had meant every word. Still, the Fishers' biggest gift was an intangible one, impossible to show but priceless in value.

Jennie felt something move against her leg under the table. She bent down to peer under the tablecloth. Scout was sitting there.

"Well, hello," she said in a loud whisper to him. "You know you shouldn't be in here."

His dark eyes gleamed as he looked up at her.

"Yes, it has been the best year ever, hasn't it? I'm grateful, too."

He rested his face on her knee. She smiled and reached down to scratch behind his ears.

"Thank you," she said. "Merry Christmas to you, too."

About the Author

CYNTHIA KELLER is the author of *An Amish Christmas*
and *A Plain & Fancy Christmas*. She lives in Connect-
icut with her husband and two children.

cynthiakeller.com

About the Type

This book was set in Goudy, a typeface designed by Frederic William Goudy (1865–1947). Goudy began his career as a bookkeeper, but devoted the rest of his life to the pursuit of "recognized quality" in a printing type.

Goudy was produced in 1914 and was an instant bestseller for the foundry. It has generous curves and smooth, even color. It is regarded as one of Goudy's finest achievements.